Jake

Gavin Kerst was born in 2000. He grew up in Johannesburg, South Africa but now lives in Sydney, Australia where he is enrolled in university and studying development planning. Ever since he completed a small writing project in high school, he had dreamed of writing his own book, and now that dream has come to life in his debut book of *Jake Raven and The Heists of Opulence.*

Jake Raven And The Heists Of Opulence

Gavin Kerst

ISBN: 978-0-6450491-0-7

Copyright © Gavin Kerst 2020

The right of Gavin Kerst to be identified as the author of this work has been asserted by him in accordance with the Copyright Act 1968.

All rights reserved. No part of this publication may be reproduced, stored in or introduced into a retrieval system, or transmitted, in any form, or by any means (electronic, mechanical, photocopying, recording or otherwise) without the prior written permission of the author. Any person who does any unauthorized act in relation to this publication may be liable to criminal prosecution and civil claims for damages.

This book is sold subject to the condition that it shall not, by way of trade or otherwise, be lent, re-sold, hired out, or otherwise circulated without the author's prior consent in any form of binding or cover than in which it is published and without a similar condition including this condition being imposed on the subsequent purchaser.

This is a work of fiction. Names, characters, places and incidents are either the product of the author's imagination or are used fictitiously, and any resemblance to actual persons, living or dead, businesses, companies, events or locales is entirely coincidental.

Instagram @gavin.kerst

Book cover done by Bookcoversart.com

1. Breaking News

BREAKING NEWS: Four suspects were arrested this morning following the armed robbery of Sydney's George Street Jewellers. An estimated $100 000 worth of jewellery was stolen from the store. The owner claimed to have secretly activated the silent alarm during the robbery, which triggered an immediate response from close by local law enforcement. A chase commenced down George Street, through Circular Quay and the Botanical Gardens, but the suspects were caught at the water's edge of Mrs Macquarie's Chair; however, the stolen jewellery was nowhere to be found.

2.　Dana's Theory

Jake Raven wasn't overly different to other teenagers his age, but what separated Jake from the others was that he had a passion for archaeology and more specifically, treasure. He had been obsessed with the idea of finding hidden treasure ever since he learnt about the successes of famous pirates as a young boy. Even though stealing jewellery from a store is not nearly the same as finding hidden treasure, it was only natural for Jake to be intrigued by the latest release of breaking news he had read a couple hours earlier. He had no doubt that his best friend Dana would mention it upon their next meetup.

At the end of third period, the school bell rang indicating that it was time for lunch. Jake made his way to the table he and Dana usually sit at, underneath the trees, next to the basketball courts, and well beyond the childish and obnoxious seventh grade hangout area. Jake found that his familiar, long-haired, blonde friend was waiting at the table already, so he joined her.

"Did you see the latest news report this morning?" Dana asked.

Jake and Dana had a way of starting conversation on a topic of interest almost always immediately, not often feeling the need for greetings or pleasantries between themselves. It was one of the many reasons why they had been best friends for such a long time, they were always mentally in sync like that.

"You mean the daily weather news report? Yeah I saw it," Jake said jokingly, clearly hiding his interest in this very conversation which he predicted just a few moments earlier.

"Funny," Dana said, clearly not amused. "You know I mean the one about the robbery on George Street."

"Yes I do, and I think it was rather stupid of them to attempt robbery in broad daylight in one of Sydney's busiest streets and shops."

"That's very true, but did you read the part about Mrs Macquarie's Chair and the unrecovered jewellery?"

"That part did intrigue me. It's hard to imagine where the suspects could have dropped off the jewellery in a hurry without anyone noticing."

"Exactly! I was also on the phone to my dad earlier and he said that there are officers searching the nearby areas for the jewellery, but nothing has turned up yet."

Dana's dad was deputy chief of police, which means that Dana often got a lot of specific and sometimes sensitive information before the general public did. Even though that often went against police guidelines, Dana was simply too interested in her dad's police involvement for that to matter.

"That sucks but it's not like we know where the jewellery is," Jake said.

"Well, it just so happens that I have a theory which could lead us to the jewellery," Dana said.

"You're kidding," Jake said.

"Nope," Dana said confidently.

"Go on then. Tell me what your theory is."

Dana pulled out her phone to show Jake a map of the Botanical Gardens which was just behind Mrs Macquarie's Chair, the location of arrest.

"Do you see that the run from Circular Quay to Mrs Macquarie's Chair isn't exactly straight?" Dana asked.

"Yeah, they would have to take a few turns and make their way around the main pond in order to get there," Jake said.

"And that's where I think the suspects dropped the jewellery."

"No way. There's too much public exposure there, they would've been seen doing that."

"Not necessarily. The first corner they had to take around the pond is blind, plus there's trees and shrubbery everywhere. I think they had just enough time to drop the jewellery in the pond unnoticed."

Jake thought this theory was a bit too ambitious, but he decided to go on with the conversation anyway since he was intrigued by where it would lead.

"So, are you saying the jewellery is now lying at the bottom of the Botanical Gardens pond?" Jake asked.

"Yes, but it's not that simple. Every Friday night at 10 o'clock, the pond gets cleaned. The water from the pond gets sent to a close by wastewater facility whilst simultaneously being replaced by new, clean water. It's a smooth process which is hard to notice since it's a subsurface operation. My point is that I think there is at least one more person working this jewellery job, and he or she is probably on the inside of that wastewater facility. All that person has to do is sit pretty and wait for the clean-up process to suck the jewellery up the pipe, and straight to them," Dana explained.

"Wow," Jake said, quite impressed by Dana's elaborate thinking. "There is one thing that doesn't add up though. Why would the arrested suspects fall for a plan like that? They would have to be monumentally stupid."

"Maybe they were, or maybe the leader made it seem like an attractive plan."

"Maybe," Jake said in deep thought. "Let's say you're right, why not just tell your dad to test if your theory is right?"

"My dad thinks it's a long shot."

"Dana, *I* think it's a long shot. What if you're wrong?"

"If I'm wrong then we look like a couple of idiots, but if I'm right, then the *police* would look like idiots and we'd be heroes making the local news."

"I'm not too sure we would make local news. I think the police would try to cover up that kind of mistake."

"That may be true, but it would still be awesome."

"I suppose that's also true," Jake said, nodding in agreement.

"So what do you say, Jake, are you keen for a trip up to the Botanical Gardens tonight?"

Jake fell silent for a moment, pondering over this information and Dana's enthusiasm. For all the years that Jake had known Dana, Jake had witnessed her come up with some pretty crazy theories about anything and everything, and that's part of the reason why Jake was such good friends with her, because she was so interestingly and excitingly different. Most importantly, throughout their entire friendship, they had each other's backs, so he knew what he wanted to say.

Jake let out a brief sigh followed by a smile, a smile of mischief. "How is it that you always convince me to do these things?"

3. Chase

"So, let me get this straight, you made me drive you and I, with our scuba gear, from your house in the northern beaches, across the Harbour Bridge and all the way to the Botanical Gardens, just so we can go snoop around in the Botanical Gardens pond?" Jake asked.

"Yes, Jake, quite the adventure isn't it?" Dana said cheekily.

"Yeah, right," Jake said nonchalantly, even though they both knew there was a chance Dana could be right and the situation could be serious.

A year ago when Jake and Dana had eagerly got their scuba diving license, Jake had never thought he'd use his gear on the inside of a pond. To be fair, they didn't *have to* use it, but they figured it would make searching the entire pond a lot quicker.

"Well we're lucky that it's late and no one is around," Jake said as they were getting out of his car.

"Why is that? You think we'll look suspicious?" Dana asked.

"No, I just think we would look like morons given the current setting."

"But Jake, don't you always look like a moron?" Dana asked jokingly.

"Now that just hurts my feelings," Jake said before pretending to express sadness.

Dana chuckled. "Let's just get to this pond, shall we?"

"Good idea."

As they walked past the shrubbery, tall trees and beyond the blind corner Dana had mentioned before, they noticed water movement in the pond.

"Um, what's going on?" Jake asked in suspicion.

"It looks like the cleaning process has already started, but it's not due to start for another twenty minutes," Dana said.

Jake and Dana had planned to arrive considerably early to leave enough time to search the pond, so something was off.

"Well that means either the cleaning process is legitimately early tonight...or someone else is here," Jake said. "Ok, you dive in quickly and check if you can see anything. I'll go to the entrance of the wastewater facility to see if anyone is there," he said in quick reaction.

"Ok, be careful."

Jake gave out a brief smile and a nod of assurance to Dana before he set off.

As Jake was nearing the entrance of the wastewater facility, he noticed it was slightly below ground level and quite inconspicuous, which made sense since it's not a very pleasing site, especially on the edge of the botanical gardens. As he was about to descend the few stairs that led to the entrance door, he saw the handle move and the door started to open. Jake instinctively dove across an embankment to his left, getting out of visibility just in time. Jake didn't know what made him do that, the person walking through the door could have easily been a worker, but Jake thought his decision was appropriate given the situation he and Dana were in.

A man wearing grey overalls and a cap walked out. Jake thought that was odd considering caps are useless at night, almost like the man had the intention of being hidden. But Jake's attention was more drawn to the two backpacks the man was carrying over his shoulders. They looked heavy, as well as drenched and dripping with water.

At that moment Dana stepped out of the pond. The man saw Dana and suddenly stopped. It was as if time was running in slow motion and all three of them could sense what was wrong in their own situation. The man bolted towards the street and Jake sprinted after him.

"Jake!" Dana called concerningly.

"Just call the police and try to follow us!" Jake shouted back in return whilst still continuing his chase.

Jake was gaining on the man and Jake was determined not to let him get to the car he was running towards. Jake got within a couple of meters and made a dive. The dive was almost miscalculated but luckily, Jake still managed to snatch his opponent's ankles causing him to fall to the ground in an instant. Within in no time they were both on their feet, standing face to face, circling one another.

"What are you planning on doing, kid?" the man asked.

"I could ask you the same thing," Jake said just before lunging toward the man and quickly throwing a punch.

Even with a couple of backpacks around his shoulder, the man had quick reflexes and managed to dodge Jake, and kick him behind the knee, causing him to double over. The man then used this opportunity to aggressively shove Jake towards the ground. This gave Jake's adversary enough time to get into his car, but Jake wasn't giving up. He sprung up from the floor and managed to swiftly open the passenger door and lunge inside just before the man accelerated. As Jake did that he shoved the man up against the car door, causing the car to violently jerk left and right from the unsettled movements of the steering wheel. Jake managed to firmly strangle his opponent, causing him to gasp for breath. But Jake couldn't do much more since he looked out the window and saw they needed to make a sharp left turn, or they would head straight into a building. So he yanked the steering wheel to the left just in time with the sound of screeching rear tires. This gave the man space to work with and he managed to pull out a pistol.

Jake reacted quickly and knocked his opponent's arm against the dashboard, causing the pistol to slip from his grasp. Jake grabbed the pistol and pointed it towards the man, and the struggling between them stopped, although they were still streaking past the surrounding buildings from the speed of the car.

"Stop the car or I'll shoot you," Jake said.

Jake wouldn't have actually shot him, but Jake tried to make that sentence sound as menacing as possible for persuasion.

"As you wish," the man said.

He pulled the handbrake and ripped the steering wheel to the right, quickly rotating the car ninety degrees. He rapidly opened the car door, smoothly jumped out and rolled onto the concrete somewhat unscathed. Jake was not as fortunate. The car continued sliding and slammed into a curb, forcing the car into a violent roll, landing straight into the ocean.

4. Discovery

Jake woke up in a coughing fit on the grass and with a throbbing headache. Dana was sitting next to him with a look of concern on her face. There were also two paramedics crouching next to Dana, and Jake saw a few police cars parked behind an ambulance.

"What happened?" Jake asked Dana as he was sitting up.

"Thank you for the help guys," Dana said to the two paramedics. "Do you mind if I have a minute alone with him?"

"Sure thing, Dana," one of them said.

"You know them?" Jake asked Dana.

"My dad has more than just law enforcement connections. Anyway, while you were having your fun with the thief, I had to follow the chase like you said. On my chase, I managed to call my dad and give him the basic details. On his way he called these paramedics for me, while *he* also came in rapid pursuit as well."

"How did I end up here?"

"Well, luckily my dad and his colleagues arrived quickly. As I was reaching the water, there happened to be another three men looking for something in the water as well, not even mildly concerned about the crash and that a fellow civilian could be drowning, but the original suspect had long gone. Luckily, as I rushed in to rescue you, my dad and his colleagues arrived with sirens blaring and all, so those men hastily made their way out too," Dana explained. "When I rescued you from the water, you were unconscious. The paramedics had to resuscitate you because you were unconscious due to a violent knock from the impact of the crash. That would also explain the swelling on your head," Dana said.

Jake sat quietly as he was taking it all in. This was not how he had expected the night to go and he was sure glad he had Dana with him.

"Thank you for rescuing me," he said while gently grabbing Dana's hand.

Dana gave out an affectionate smile.

"What are friends for?" Dana asked rhetorically. "But you know what I find amazing?"

"What?"

"You chased after that guy without a second thought, knowing there could be consequences. How did you pluck up the courage to do that?"

"Well, a while ago you told me something that changed my perspective on things."

"What was that?"

"While we were playing in the mixed basketball championship final together, I was playing terribly and I definitely thought our team was going to lose because of me," Jake said. "Then you came to me and said, 'If you don't believe in yourself, who else will?' I always carry that believe with me now."

Dana smiled at the memory, a key moment in their friendship. And then they sat together in silence, just for a few minutes, reflecting over the crazy sequence of events they had just been through.

Thirty minutes later, Dana's dad, Ryan Evans, came strolling towards them. He had a muscular build, formed from years of lifting heavy weights in the gym, and refined by keeping his nutrition and cardio in check. He looked tough, but also sophisticated due to his smoothly combed brown hair. He was far from the stereotypical police officer.

"How's the head, Jake?" Ryan asked.

"It's eased up now. I'm thankful Dana was there when she was, Mr Evans."

"Well, we appreciate your effort in this," Ryan said. "And Jake, how long have we known each other? Years, so please, call me Ryan."

"Will do, Ryan," Jake said.

"That's more like it," Ryan said, exuding a gentle smile. "Anyway, when I saw those three men hovering in the water, I wanted to check out what they were searching for. So, I sent a couple of my colleagues down there and we discovered something that I know you might like. You better come take a look at this."

"Do you have the authority to let us do that?" Jake asked.

"This isn't a crime scene. Anyone can look at it," Ryan said.

"Ok then, let's go check it out," Jake said.

Two minutes later, Jake and Dana were swimming down to the harbour floor near the site of the crash. It wasn't too deep, but Ryan suggested they bring their scuba gear due to the prospect of Jake's interest. As Jake and Dana approached the underwater harbour floor, they saw something that seemed a little out of place. Lying at the bottom was a rectangular slab of concrete, about two meters long, one meter wide and three inches thick. Jake noticed some sort of indentation on the top. They had to brush some sand and algae away to get a clear look at it all. Now they could see that on top of the concrete was a carved design of an anchor with diagonal lines behind it. Below that a small message read, *'My Fortune Awaits,'* and above those words, *'Joseph Harrison'*. On the side, there was a final phrase that read, *'Zl ynfg fgbc,'* which obviously didn't make sense to Jake or Dana. Jake pointed up to Dana, signalling that he wanted to surface and discuss this discovery.

As they resurfaced, Jake ripped out his scuba breather and excitingly said, "Dana, this is absolutely insane!"

"This discovery is more significant than I thought based on that reaction," Dana stated.

"Do you know who Joseph Harrison was?" Jake asked eagerly.

"You've mentioned him a couple times, a famous pirate."

"Not just a famous pirate. To this day, he's the most successful pirate to have ever graced this planet."

"Why was he so successful?"

"Dana, let me tell you a little story."

5. Joseph Harrison

Joseph Harrison was known for many things and was arguably the most successful pirate of all time. His accomplishments rivalled the likes of Sir Francis Drake, Edward England or even the notorious Henry Every. Joseph Harrison; however, stole the three most prized artefacts in the world that were secured in the most ruthless and indisputable facilities possible. These included the *Cross of Faith* from Scotland, the *Ring of Valour* from South Africa and the *Sword of Capacity* from Russia. Harrison successfully managed to obtain these artefacts in a time window of no more than two years, ending in 1929, the kind of pace that was deemed impossible for such times. Harrison did what no one else could; a feat reaching the highest degrees of prosperity, and from that point on, would forever be known as *The Heists Of Opulence.*

6.   Deciphering

"Wow, that's incredible," Dana said as they were walking out of the water. "Now I understand why it's such a big deal."

Ryan was in discussion with his colleagues next to the police cars, so he missed this exciting conversation.

"Yes, it's a *huge* deal Dana," Jake said.

"But why is this here?" Dana asked.

"When Harrison died, his treasure vanished along with him, including the artefacts from *The Heists of Opulence*. I bet anything this might be some sort of clue leading to where at least some of the treasure is."

"That might be a bit of a stretch, Jake. For something that is *this* old, someone would have discovered it by now because the majority of the harbour floor has been mapped."

"The mapping is for undulations and surface changes on the harbour floor, not every object unless they're easily distinctive."

"Ok, so what makes you think this is a clue left by Harrison?"

"Although Harrison travelled the world to complete his ridiculous feats, he still came from Sydney and it's no secret that he loved it here. His famous grave is literally a few kilometres away from this spot. I bet in his days of retirement he wanted to hide his treasure and plant some sort of clue that someone could potentially stumble across so he could share the glory in his own uniquely formulated way," Jake explained.

"I guess that might not be a total stretch," Dana admitted.

"The only problem is we don't really have any direction because I still didn't deduct anything from what we've just seen," Jake said.

"I think I may have an idea that could help us," Dana said.

"Go on then," Jake said.

"What if the phrase on the side is some sort of code?"

***

Later that night Jake and Dana decided that what they originally wanted to do; catch the jewellery thief, was to be handed over to the Ryan and the police. They spotted a missed clue and acted on it. From where they ended up, they weren't any further than the police, which they thought was convenient due to their desire to focus on their recent discovery.

The next morning they made their way to the State Library of New South Wales.

"So, why are we going to the State Library?" Jake asked.

"We're going because it's the oldest library in Australia and it's been around since long before Harrison was around. It has all sorts of information and public records," Dana said.

"Yeah, but we could just get what we want online," Jake said.

"I know, but it's a lot easier having the tangible objects. That way we can shuffle around bits and pieces and make copies if we need to. Plus, sometimes not all of the sources are made available online anyway," Dana said.

This was a classic dynamic of Jake and Dana. If Jake was passionate about something and he wanted to explore deeper, Dana would always find a way to help him.

They were just getting off the train at Martin Place, the closest train station to the State Library. As they were walking up the stairs to street level, they emerged with the sight of skyscrapers and constant movement of traffic and people; the ever-bustling central business district of Sydney.

As they were making their way through the crowds, Dana said, "So, once we're inside, we can split up since we need to find anything related to different code languages and anything related to the life of Joseph Harrison."

"Sounds good to me."

Astonishment filled Jake's mind as they stepped into the library. There were countless amounts of bookshelves containing all sorts of literature, several rows of tables and cubicles, plenty of electrical facilities like computers or printers along the outskirts and much of the three-storey library was occupied by heavily concentrated university students, giving off a huge aura of professionalism.

Jake went to seek out any sources of information on Harrison while Dana went to look for books on code languages. Luckily, both topics were very specific, so they took no longer than ten minutes to gather what they wanted.

They found a quiet desk secluded in a corner since obviously they wanted to keep their little project a secret. They then spent an additional ten minutes reading through what they had. Dana was having difficulties trying to rapidly learn variations of code and match them to the phrase on the concrete slab that they had a photograph of. Jake was looking through Harrison's history in an attempt to find any other clues related to Harrison's post-life treasure plans.

"Ok, I'm not having any luck here," Dana said frustratingly. "What about you?"

"These papers are essentially in-depth essays about Harrison's history. So far I haven't found anything major, but I did find one thing," Jake said.

"What's that?"

"According to these statements here, Harrison always had a specific phrase he used time and time again, kind of like a motto, which I somehow didn't know about," Jake said.

"Ok, but what's the motto?"

"*My Fortune Awaits*," Jake said dramatically.

"That's the same phrase that was on the concrete slab!" Dana said excitingly.

"Exactly," Jake agreed. "It makes sense that it's there because of the famous significance, but I also think it was left there as a message, like we're on the right track."

"Do you think it has anything to do with the design of the anchor and diagonal lines behind it?"

"No, that's just his sigil. Every pirate back then had a sigil and that was his. It doesn't necessarily relate to what we're looking for."

"Alright. Good work. Let's continue for longer to see what else comes up," Dana instructed.

Jake nodded and they both put their heads down to get back to work.

Fifteen minutes later, Dana's frustration was growing but Jake had a smile on his face.

"What's that cheeky smile about?" Dana asked.

"I found something you might like," Jake admitted.

"Go on then," Dana said impatiently to Jake's amusement.

"There's actually some photographs of evidence showing old secret letters that Harrison used to send to his acquaintances. According to these statements, nothing dramatic has been revealed in the letters shown, but it does say what form of code it was in," Jake said. "He wrote these letters in a code called ROT13; an ancient type of substitution cipher."

Dana rapidly flicked to the index page in the textbook she was using. She then flicked further forward in the book to a page containing information on ROT13. As she did that, she asked, "So, you think that phrase on the side of the concrete slab is also in ROT13?"

"It would be my bet," Jake said confidently.

"Jake this is really simple. All we need to do is match up the letters to form the original phrase."

After about thirty seconds she said, "Ok, I've got it. It says, '*My Last Stop*'."

"That could mean a bunch of different things; his last heist destination, his last place of residence, his last boat..." Jake said.

"What if it's literal?" Dana asked.

"What do you mean by that?"

"What if he means his *literal* last stop?"

Jake gasped as if he just struck an epiphany.

"His grave..."

7. Riddle

As Jake and Dana rushed their way out of the State Library and back onto the busy streets of the central business district, Jake said, "It makes perfect sense. Last night we were literally discussing that Harrison loved it here and his grave is close by."

"Exactly. Do you know how to get there?" Dana said.

"Of course I do, I've been there before."

"Ok great, but what are we doing once we get there? It's not like we can just dig up his grave. We don't have the authority for that."

"I don't think we need to dig up his grave at all," Jake said dramatically.

Dana seemed very intrigued by Jake's confidence, so they immediately commenced their trip to the graveyard. On the train to Edgecliff Station, Dana was resting her head on Jake's shoulder and gazing at Jake's shoes.

"What is it with you and your red indoor soccer boots?" Dana asked. "They don't match your trademark chinos and sweatshirt at all."

Jake chuckled. "We've been over this numerous times. They are insanely comfortable and allow me to move faster than any other shoe," he said. "Besides, you have an obsession with your black leather jacket and black boots, what's with that?"

Dana shrugged her head and said, "It looks cool."

Jake smiled, then looked up and suddenly realised they were arriving.

"We're here," Jake said.

"Ok let's go," Dana said as she stood up quickly with such enthusiasm that Jake always admired.

They had a fifteen-minute walk to McKell Park, another point that was next to the Sydney harbour. Harrison's grave was famously placed near the water's edge, facing the direction of the Sydney Harbour Bridge.

"Wow!" Dana said impressed. "Quite the view he has here. I wonder why the grave of a most wanted criminal was even allowed to be put here in the first place."

"I've wondered that before as well, but I'm sure his notoriously iconic status of legends bought him enough respect to grant him his grave wishes."

"That's a fair guess."

As they turned away from the view to look at Harrison's large headstone, they saw an inscription that was separated from the usual information placed on headstones.

I may be lost

*but it all goes on
beneath the quill
beyond the fall of the Sutherland
my fortune awaits.*

Dana looked perplexed and asked Jake, "So, it's some kind of poem?"

"I always thought so, but I've recently changed my mind about the nature of the poem," Jake said.

"What makes you say that?"

"Harrison was the kind of man that liked outsmarting people. I'm sure if anyone was on the trail, he would've wanted them to overlook this plain looking poem and dig up his grave, only to find dirt and bones. I've started to think that this is not just a poem, it's a riddle, pointing us somewhere."

"Well, if it is a riddle, how do we solve it?" Dana asked.

"That's our job to find out."

8. Research

The following afternoon, Jake and Dana were in Jake's bedroom, pondering over what Harrison's headstone message really meant. Dana was fiddling with a Rubik's Cube whilst looking at Jake's ocean view in deep thought. They had been discussing theories for half an hour but came up with nothing substantial.

Jake got up from his bed and said, "Ok, we know that the first two lines don't necessarily mean anything, and the last line is just Harrison dramatically using his famous motto for one final time."

"Maybe that's just what he wants us to think and throw us off the trail once again," Dana said.

"Well, I think it would be extremely difficult to leave a clue amidst those three lines. Although, maybe 'lost' has something to do with it, maybe a lost city or some sort of ruin. But then again it's not every day you come across news articles on such things," Jake said.

Dana let out a brief sigh and leant over Jake's balcony.

"Even so, I think you're right. It must be within the third and fourth lines," Dana said.

"Alright, so we've already discussed that 'beneath the quill' seems strange. It doesn't make much sense. I'm sure the 'quill' has got to be something else," Jake said.

"And then 'Sutherland' has a literal meaning of 'southern land', so the fourth line could point to a fallen country in the southern hemisphere, but that only narrows down half of the world."

"Ok, how about this?" Jake said. "I'll do some research tonight and I'll let you know what I come up with in the morning."

"Don't be ridiculous, I'll stay over and do some research with you."

Jake sat down at his desk and retrieved a chair from the neighbouring dining room so Dana could sit with him.

Six hours later it was eleven o'clock at night and Dana was already asleep on Jake's bed, and Jake was still sitting at his desk, rubbing his eyes and running his hands through his messy brown hair in exhaustion. He heard his front door open, but he knew it was just his mom arriving home from a late night's work. Jake convinced himself to do another ten minutes of research before he crashed, because he felt his energy levels depleting.

Dana woke up at six o'clock and found Jake drinking coffee on his balcony, cheerfully admiring the view.

"What are you smirking about?" she asked.

"I figured it out," Jake said confidently.

"What? How? When?" Dana asked excitingly.

Jake laughed as he was really enjoying this moment.

"Well, after I went through numerous fallen cities in the southern hemisphere, anything that could relate to the word 'quill,' and pretty much every article on the internet, I stumbled across something just before I went to sleep."

"What was it?"

"I found a waterfall in New Zealand called *Sutherland* Falls, and that waterfall is sourced by a lake that's called Lake *Quill*."

Dana laughed, but it was a laugh of surprise and impression.

"So, Harrison is directing us to New Zealand," Dana said. "But why would he lead us there?

"I don't know. There's no written records about Harrison with Lake Quill or Sutherland Falls. I guess he thought it was just a *really* good hiding place."

"I guess so," Dana said. "It's time to book a flight."

9. Arrival

The following afternoon, Jake was in his room packing the necessities for the flight he and Dana were intending to take the next day. Jake didn't have any concern on travelling to New Zealand, mostly due to the fact he and Dana were days away from school break. Dana on the other hand, had very strict parents, not to mention Ryan being deputy chief of police, so she was having difficulties.

Fortunately, she managed to persuade them due to the mention of the potential of discovering something very unique and valuable.

Regardless of the fact that Ryan would have no jurisdiction overseas, Jake did think it might have been a good idea to bring Ryan along because of his police training, and he could've helped them out financially, but police officers, especially deputy chiefs, don't go around chasing treasure, so it made logical sense that he didn't come. Jake and Dana agreed to call Ryan if there proved to be alarming trouble along the way.

The next morning, Jake and Dana took a taxi to the airport for their early five o'clock flight. They weren't fussed by waking up early because they were excited about what they had ahead of themselves. However, Jake hated flying. He hated the cramped seats in economy class, the not-so-desirable food and especially, the turbulence.

"Jake, you know that statistically speaking, planes are much safer than cars?" Dana asked in an attempt of reassurance half an hour into the flight.

"Those statistics don't apply when I'm the one that's driving," Jake said irritably.

Dana laughed. They had been on a few flights together before, but this behaviour was always amusing to her.

"Just wake me up when we get there," Jake said.

"Will do," Dana said, while still smiling in amusement.

Jake only ended up sleeping for about an hour which got them about halfway through the flight. He then managed to watch a bit of '*Indiana Jones and the Kingdom of the Crystal Skull,*' which he had seen about five times before, but he still considered it an effective distraction. They had a bumpy landing in Christchurch which Jake obviously didn't like, and they then had to take a transferring flight on a smaller plane to the quiet town of Glenorchy.

"Finally!" Jake said as they were walking off the second plane.

"Yeah, I agree," Dana said. "Let's go get our bags and our rental car."

It didn't take them long to get their bags and the keys for their rental car because Glenorchy airport was small and not very busy. Their rental car was a Mitsubishi Lancer; a car Jake had always wanted to drive. Dana knew there were cheaper options available, but she didn't say anything because she was amused by Jake's enjoyment, a stark contrast to what he was feeling just thirty minutes before. The drive to their accommodation was only about fifteen minutes and they spent a lot of it in silence admiring the striking blue coloured water bodies, and the never-ending mountain ranges covered by greenery. They arrived at a small wooden house overlooking the alluring site of Lake Wakatipu.

"Wow, it's beautiful," Dana said, stepping out of the car. "Remind me again why you chose this location."

"Well, Glenorchy isn't far from Sutherland falls and it has shops for basic supplies if we need them. I thought that criteria was suitable."

Dana eyed Jake a little suspiciously.

"And I may have liked the view," Jake admitted.

"Ah, I thought so," Dana said.

"Dana, we're on an adventure. We may as well go all out."

"No arguments here," Dana said. "Let's get settled in."

Jake and Dana didn't spend long in their new house. They unpacked their bags, freshened up, briefly admired the view once again, and then drove to the small shopping area of Glenorchy. They got themselves easy-to-carry and quick-to-consume groceries from the central general store and then cruised along the quiet streets, investigating where all the other stores were, since they needed to get some camping supplies.

"Harrison sure picked a good place to hide his treasure," Dana said, admiring the isolation of Glenorchy.

"Too right, a three-day trail walk just to get to the falls, it's no wonder nobody has found the treasure yet," Jake said.

"Regardless of the scenery, it's going to be a long three days considering our situation.

"Three days in the lush greenery with my sarcastic comments, what could go wrong?" Jake asked cheekily.

Dana eyed Jake amusingly and grabbed his shoulder and said, "Absolutely nothing, Jakey."

"I hate it when you call me that."

"I know."

After they got some camping supplies, they drove to the nearest carpark to Sutherland Falls since they weren't allowed any vehicles on the trail, but when they got there, there was a sign that said, *'Attraction closed, visitations prohibited during this time.'*

Jake looked at Dana and asked, "Is that going to stop us?"

"Not a chance."

10. Surprise

The trail was filled with tall trees, dense vegetation and various organisms of wildlife, most of which they could hear but not see, all the while they could see a vast range of mountains in the distance beyond the trees.

"If these were different circumstances, I'd totally spend more time on this trail. It's so beautiful and peaceful," Jake said.

"It really is, but we've got a long way to go so there's still a lot of time to admire it," Dana said.

"That's true."

They continued walking until nightfall. They set up camp on a small clearing on the side of the trail. It had enough space for a tent and a whole range of camping utilities, but they packed light, so they didn't need much of the space.

"You know," Jake started while sitting on his sleeping bag, "If I wake up with a spider or something crawling on my face, I'm really going to regret not bringing a tent."

"And who's fault would that be?" Dana asked laughing.

"Mine," Jake admitted. "But I still stand by my decision because heavy equipment would only slow us down."

"No objections here."

They slept well through the night and continued walking at a strong pace the next day. They came across a wooden bridge going over a stream coming from a small waterfall.

"Oh look, a waterfall," Dana said. "I think we've found our treasure," she said sarcastically.

"According to my prior research, I believe that waterfall is called Giant Gate Falls, a bit ironic really," Jake said.

"Certainly," Dana said. "The water looks so inviting though, it's crystal clear."

"Do you want to take a quick dip?"

"I'd love to, but it's gonna take too long. Let's keep going."

Jake certainly didn't disagree, he wanted to get to the treasure as soon as possible. They continued walking through dense forest and along steep undulations throughout the day. This day was not unlike the day before, they kept a calm and steady pace and had a seamless sleep through the night. However, the third day presented some difficulties. They had to walk along an extensive cliffside with a narrow pathway where there was very little room for error.

"You'd think maybe there would be a simpler path, one that was a lot flatter than this," Jake said, cautiously making his way along the cliffside.

"Yeah, I suppose the authorities wanted to leave the environment as undisturbed as possible," Dana said. "It does make it difficult though."

"Luckily we don't have long to go with this section, let's keep moving."

It took them a few minutes to get to the end of the cliffside and when they did, there was a sigh of relief from both of them. They were then led on a steady downward slope towards more dense greenery. Once the path flattened out they started jogging to make up for the bit of time they lost.

Jake pulled out his phone to take a look at a map of the trail they were on and said, "I don't know if I'm reading the map wrong, which is highly unlikely, or if we're actually not that far from the waterfall."

"That makes sense because you did say it would take three full days. We're just going *slightly* quicker than the average person due to the circumstances."

"Yeah, but I'm still a bit surpri—"

A loud bang cut off Jake's sentence. It almost sounded like an explosion. They saw birds flutter out of the forest in the near distance.

Dana worryingly looked at Jake and said, "I wonder what that was."

"I don't know. Let's go check it out. But let's cut off the path amongst the trees and stay low. It could be anything."

They crept amongst the greenery for a few minutes and after about two hundred metres, they thought they could hear the faint sound of voices. Jake stopped and looked at Dana. She gave him a nod, indicating she was all good to go on. They crept for about another fifty meters and the voices were getting louder and they thought they could hear the sound of running water. They finally spotted two men in the centre of the trail wearing khaki coloured clothing and black utility vests, each holding an assault rifle.

"Why are we even guarding this? It's not like anyone will come down here anyway," the one said.

"Because if Walker manages to find his treasure, we'll each be getting a huge payout. Besides, it could be worse," the other said.

Jake gave Dana a look of concern. Again, she gave him a nod of assurance and then made an arching motion with her left hand, as if to tell Jake to cut further into the bush to go around the guards. He understood. After making their way past the guards, they noticed the sound of the water was getting even louder than before, and they could hear more voices too. After about another forty meters, they spotted the waterfall through the trees. As they were getting closer, they had to make their way over a blind rise and down a small embankment.

They weren't prepared for what they saw next. There were about thirty men scattered around a large network of tents, camping utilities and an array of heavy-duty tools and equipment, all part of a very extensive operation.

Jake turned to Dana and whispered, "I think we might have a problem."

11. Restraint

"This is insane," Dana said. "Somehow, these guys know about the treasure too."

"The only question is how."

"Maybe they saw the concrete slab as well, or maybe there's another set of clues entirely."

"Maybe," Jake said with his brain running a million miles an hour. "What matters now is discussing our options. We could find a way to sneak by them and search for the treasure ourselves, which would be tricky. We could try and work with them, which would also be tricky. Or, we could call this a day and go home to eliminate risk."

"We didn't come all this way just to quit," Dana said. "I say we try to work the situation ourselves. This group doesn't seem like the cooperative type."

"Ok, let's go further around all this and get a better understanding of our environment."

They made a loop around the left line of tents. Once they got around, they started to feel the spray of the waterfall and finally saw it in all its glory. The only reason why the area wasn't soaked is because the waterfall uniquely thinned out at the bottom, slowly flowing downwards into a small stream.

"Wow, it's amazing," Dana said.

"Yeah, it's the tallest waterfall in New Zealand, reaching five hundred and eighty meters at its peak."

"Anyway, back to the task at hand. I think these guys are searching in the wrong place. We need to find a way to get past them. And we also need to find a way *up*," Jake said.

"Yeah, but the actual process of doing that is gonna be a problem since we can't attract any attention," Dana said.

"I know. Let's try make it around to the other side and attempt to expand our perspective on this place."

"Ok."

But as they turned around, there was a blur of motion in front of them, and suddenly, they were knocked unconscious, hitting the ground hard.

***

Jake slowly regained his consciousness, but he could feel he was in danger. When he opened his eyes, he could see he was in a large tent that had a couple stand-up tables with various tools, and he was restrained to a plastic chair. It was very difficult for him to move. A man was ominously sitting with his back to Jake, at the tent's entrance. Something about him seemed familiar to Jake.

"Where's my friend?" Jake asked.

"Oh look, he's awake," the man said.

"I said, where's my friend?" Jake asked a little more defiantly.

"She's...been taken care of," the man said calmly.

Jake was wondering what that meant. He was starting to get angry.

"Look, my friend and I were just trying to complete Milford Track. It's a trail we've been wanting to do for a long time, and we weren't gonna turn back just because there was some stupid sign at the beginning saying we couldn't," Jake said, hoping this was convincing.

The man had an evil laugh. "I'm sure that's the case," the man said sarcastically.

The man turned around and Jake gasped.

"You?!" Jake said. It was the same man he tried chasing down at the Botanical Gardens; the jewellery thief.

"Yeah, I knew you'd recognise me," the man said. "Anyway, what brings you here, *Jake Raven*?"

Jake cursed silently. The man must have seen Jake's wallet with his identification and all his other belongings to go with it. His anger was growing larger.

"It's like I said, my friend and I were just walking the trail," Jake said, somehow managing to stay calm.

"Do you think I'm a fool?" the man asked.

"Maybe," Jake said with a clear change of tone. "You looked like an amateur the other night. I almost had you."

"Yeah, but I still got away. You didn't achieve anything other than the fact that you found the very concrete slab we were trying to remove, and now you're here, hassling *me*."

This was surprising to Jake. This guy was working two different jobs that night, stealing the jewellery *and* using other people to try remove the concrete slab. But Jake was also frustrated. He knew this interaction was going south, and quickly.

"Ok, why don't you just let me go?" Jake asked. "Then I'll be out of your way, *with* my friend."

"No, we're quite done here," the man said. Then he turned around and left.

Jake was desperately trying to break free of the ropes that were restraining him, but there was no point, they were too tight. But then he saw there were some tools lying on a couple stand-up tables against the side of the tent. Jake was right, maybe the man was a fool.

12. Scheme

It had taken a painstakingly slow three minutes for Jake to make it to the tables at the side of the tent. He somehow managed to hop his way there on the chair he was restrained to without falling over, although his wrists were hurting like hell from rope burn, and his problems were far from over. It wasn't like he could just get up and simply grab what he needed. He also couldn't tip the table onto the floor since the people outside would hear the commotion. His task had to be done delicately. As Jake was searching for a solution, he saw a knife that was resting by the edge on one of the tables. After a few more hops, he got into the position he needed, but he still couldn't reach the knife. He made one final hop ninety degrees to the left, hoping he hadn't miscalculated. As he reached out, he could feel the handle of the knife on his fingertips. He painfully extended further and managed to grab the knife, but it slipped from his grasp. He managed to catch it at the last moment. After his heart skipped a beat, Jake then flipped the knife over and began cutting through the rope. In no more than a minute, his hands were free, and it only took him another few seconds to undo the rope tying his feet together.

Now he needed to get out of the tent without being seen.

One problem at a time, Jake thought.

He pocketed the knife and crept up to the entrance of the tent and took a peek at his surroundings. Fortunately there was no one guarding his tent, but Jake was still concerned about getting past all those men without getting seen. He considered waiting until dark, but he needed to prioritise Dana's safety, that's if she was *alive*. Jake didn't let that thought take over, he needed to focus, and he needed to do something immediately. He spotted an elevated section of bush which was behind some of the neighbouring tents to the right but still had a good view of the operation in front of him. When Jake thought it was clear, he made a dash for it.

He made it there safely.

Jake thought about the fact that the last time he was in the bush investigating something, he and Dana got knocked out.

To get that concern out of his mind, he started taking in his surroundings, trying to figure out where Dana might be. What caught his eye was the largest tent of the operation, directly opposite from where he was crouching. Just outside the entrance of the tent was the man that was interrogating Jake just a few minutes earlier. He was overseeing the whole operation and had the tendency to bark unnecessarily loud orders. He must have been the man in charge, otherwise known as

Walker, or so Jake thought according to the two guards he and Dana had to sneak past earlier.

Just as Jake was figuring out a way to get to the tent, he spotted a military style Jeep coming down the main trail on his left. As the driver was getting out, one of the other men was walking towards him and jokingly said, "You know, you could really do some harmful environmental degradation taking that Jeep down here."

"Oh really? What a shame," the driver said, before they shortly released diabolical laughter.

"Aren't you gonna turn the car off?" the one man asked.

"No it doesn't matter. I'm just dropping these supplies off and then I'm out of here," the driver said.

Jake really didn't like these guys and their lack of appreciation for the environment, but at least he had come up with a plan. He didn't even take the time to consider how good of an idea this was, he was fully committed.

The two men were unloading a large box from the car and as soon as they were out of visual range, Jake bolted towards the Jeep. He then opened the driver's door, let the handbrake down, and then dashed to the bushes on his left. The Jeep was rolling towards the centre of the operation, but Jake didn't even take the time to look. He rapidly looped around the left line of tents and as he got to the main one, he heard a loud crash and everyone chaotically scrambled.

Walker was no longer standing guard at the tent, so Jake darted inside, and his guess was proven right, since Dana was there. Like Jake, she was restrained with ropes to a chair, but she was still unconscious. Their bags were there too. Jake quickly grabbed one of their backpacks, untied Dana, tossed her over his shoulder, and he was out of there.

13. Backtracking

Jake managed to carry Dana and one of their backpacks a long way away from the threat they just escaped from. When Jake was convinced he could take a safe rest stop, he set Dana and the backpack down in the shade. Luckily the backpack he had was the one with important documents and sufficient supply of food and water. Now that the adrenalin rush had worn off, Jake had a massive headache, most likely caused by the blow to the head. Jake had no doubt Dana would be feeling the same when she woke up. Jake was surprised that Dana hadn't been woken up from the loud commotion earlier or from being carried on a bumpy run, but he guessed that's what a concussion would do to you. Jake took out one of the bottles of water and threw some water on Dana's face.

She jumped back in to life with a loud gasp and said, "What on Earth happened?"

Jake explained the story of how they both got knocked unconscious, the interaction he had with Walker and the success of Jake's vivid escape plan.

"Wow, that's quite the story," Dana said, impressed but in slight discomfort from her headache. "Thanks for rescuing me."

Jake smiled at Dana affectionately.

"What are friends for?" Jake asked rhetorically.

Jake gave Dana a few moments to regather herself and gain some energy.

"So, what's the plan from here?" she asked Jake.

"I say we backtrack, get some more supplies and come back more prepared."

"Can we afford to do that though? Won't it take too much time?"

"By the looks of it, those guys back there aren't finding the treasure any time soon. They're digging up every square inch of dirt at the base of the waterfall. They're looking in the wrong place, it's a huge waste of time," Jake said.

"*Beneath the quill, beyond the fall of the Sutherland,*" Dana said dramatically.

"Exactly. By the time they come to their senses, we'll be right onto them," Jake said.

"Alright then," Dana said determinedly.

"But before we do anything, I think we should call your dad. I know as a police officer, or deputy chief for that matter, he doesn't have any jurisdiction here, but I would feel a lot better if he was here."

"I agree. I'll call him on the way and tell him about our situation."

Jake helped Dana to her feet, and they started making their way back to Glenorchy.

***

They fast-tracked their way back up to the beginning of the trail. It only took them a day to do so, although when they got to the car park with their Mitsubishi Lancer rental car, they were exhausted because they hadn't taken the time to sleep on the trip back.

Jake somehow managed to safely drive them back to the central general store so they could pick up extra food and water. While Jake was purchasing what they needed, Dana was outside and called her dad, Ryan, and explained the situation to him.

As Jake walked out the store he asked, "So, is he coming?"

"I don't know how he has got permission to come here so suddenly with all of his responsibilities, but yes, he's coming. He'll be here in a couple days."

"Good stuff," Jake said positively. "Now, we do have one more stop before we make our way back."

A couple minutes later they were in the hardware store and Dana asked, "So, we're buying this climbing rope and equipment because you think we might need to repel down that huge cliff face that the waterfall goes off?"

"After scoping out that waterfall, I think Harrison might be pointing us towards doing that, unless there's some sort of irregularity within the Lake or maybe a system of interconnecting caves. We actually should've thought of all the options *before* all this happened, but I guess it took seeing the actual environment for us to realise that," Jake said truthfully.

"Alright, Jakey. Let's get this show on the road."

They went back to their small wooden house overlooking Lake Wakatipu and got some good sleep, but they had an alarm set and rose in the early morning.

As Jake was getting changed into a fresh set of clothes he said, "Remind me to go for cheaper accommodation the next time we go treasure hunting. There's no point going big when we barely spend time *in* the accommodation."

"Yeah I could've told you that before we even arrived here," Dana said in amusement, although her tone suddenly changed when she thought about the trip back down. "Walking down that trail is gonna be exhausting, especially since we're still on the clock."

"Oh, I didn't tell you. We're not walking down," Jake said smiling.

"What do you mean?" Dana asked.

"Let me show you," Jake said.

A little while later they were back at the motor rental agency and they were standing in front of two dirt bikes, and Jake had a cheeky grin on his face.

"Dirt bikes?" Dana said.

"Yes," Jake said simply.

"But we're not allowed vehicles on the trail," Dana said.

"Well, Walker and his men took a bloody Jeep and all sorts of heavy equipment down there. What difference are a couple of dirt bikes gonna make? Besides, we'll try to avoid the precious vegetation where we can," Jake said.

"Jake," Dana said grabbing Jake's shoulder affectionately, "I think this is a marvellous idea."

"Then let's go."

14. Ascent

The ride back down the trail proved to be very time effective. They were swiftly cutting between the trees and vegetation, and it was a pleasure feeling the constant breeze of the wind. They would've made it to the waterfall in just a few hours, but they still had to cross that precarious narrow pathway next to the extensive cliffside.

It was too risky to ride the bikes across, so they got off to walk. It was a much more awkward process having to keep hold of the bikes and not lose them down a cliff.

"This is ridiculous," Dana said worryingly.

"I know," Jake said nervously. "Let's just keep going, keep it steady."

Step by step, they slowly made their way, and there was a big sigh of relief when they got to the other side.

They took a couple moments to settle their nerves, then got back on the bikes. They had to diverge their path since this time they wanted to be at the top of the waterfall by the lake. This also proved to be awkward because they had to ascend a steep incline and had to manoeuvre their way around rocky outcrops and delicately apply the throttle pressure on sections with loose gravel.

As they reached the top of the peak, they came across an astonishing view. They could see a vast range of mountain peaks patched with snow and expansive greenery wherever they looked. Then looking down they saw Lake Quill, which was even more striking than any online image ever illustrated. The water was a deep, deep blue, and something about it being surrounded by mountains in a crater-like shape gave it a really intimidating aura. But then they saw something else as well.

On the west side of the lake, Jake saw what looked like a familiar base of operations with an array heavy-duty tools and equipment; Walker and his men.

Jake looked at Dana and said, "Well, well, well, I guess they're not complete fools after all."

15. Cooperation

Jake and Dana were sitting behind the mountain's peak, overlooking Lake Quill and Walker's operation. They had already started discussing their options on which method of approach to take.

"Well, I think it would be pretty dumb to do anything now since there aren't many trees to cover us. There's about a ninety-nine percent chance we'll be spotted," Jake said.

"I agree," Dana said. "So we're gonna wait until dark before we start sneaking around?"

"Yeah, that seems like the most viable option," Jake said. "You ready for a stakeout, Dana?"

"As ready as I'll ever be."

Even though they had quality sleep the night before, they still had a few hours until dark, so Dana managed to nap while Jake kept watch, then after a short while, Dana offered the reverse for Jake. When Jake woke up, it was starting to get dark, so they discussed their plan of approach.

"Ok, as you mentioned before, these guys don't seem like the cooperative type, but at this point, we don't have much choice. So, we'll sneak around the edge of the peak until we create the shortest path between us and Walker's operation. Then we'll infiltrate Walker's tent and force him to negotiate with us," Jake said. "Am I missing anything?"

"Nope, it's all clear to me," Dana said. "Besides, in this situation, risks will always be presented one way or another."

"Exactly," Jake said. "You ready to go?"

"Absolutely," Dana said confidently.

They slowly crept their way around the crater-like mountain peak until they were directly behind Walker's operation. From frequent observations they had figured out which tent was Walker's and the fact that he occupied the tent alone. Fortunately for Jake and Dana, Walker's tent was at the back, overlooking the operation.

They carefully made their way down to the back of Walker's tent, making sure they didn't stand on any branches that might break noisily, and they stayed out of significant lines of sight. When they got to the back of Walker's tent, they could see his sitting silhouette through the fabric. As Walker got up and walked towards the front of the tent, Jake and Dana sensed an opportunity.

Dana quietly undid the tent's back zip and Jake silently charged inside. Jake aggressively wrapped his right arm tight around Walker's neck and used his left hand to cover Walker's mouth. There were a couple of muffled gasps but to Jake's surprise, Walker managed to flip Jake over his shoulder and Jake landed in a heap on the floor. Dana came charging in support, but Walker expertly aimed a roundhouse kick at her. She ducked quickly and swept his other leg from under him, this time causing Walker to end up on the floor.

Jake got up quickly to help Dana securely restrain Walker, but not before Walker shouted, "HELP!"

They heard a succession of footsteps, so Dana took out a knife and held it closely to Walker's throat. A few of Walker's men hurriedly appeared in the tent's entrance and aimed their assault rifles at Jake and Dana.

"What the hell is going on here?" the lead man said.

"It doesn't matter. Shoot them!" Walker demanded.

The lead man remained stationary, cautiously eyeing Jake and Dana.

Jake put his hands up in an attempt of reassurance and said, "We're just trying to find the treasure, let us work together and we won't give you any more trouble."

The man was slowly lowering his weapon, realising they weren't under much direct threat.

"Didn't you hear me? Shoot them!" Walker said aggressively.

"No. Killing them, at least *right now*, would be a bit extreme," the man said, then looking at his other acquaintances. "They're obviously very invested in this treasure, so stand down, they can work alongside us."

Walker couldn't argue because he knew he needed his team, so Dana pocketed the knife and the situation had calmed.

Once Walker had angrily left the tent, Dana said to the man, "Thanks for not killing us."

"It's alright. Name's Bradley," the man said, firmly shaking Jake and Dana's hands.

"You can work with us, but don't even think about retaliating, you will regret it," Bradley said in a very menacing tone, vastly different to the politeness he had just displayed moments ago.

Bradley was tall, had a buzz cut, and an athletic build with biceps bulging underneath his shirt. He was not the kind of guy to be messed with.

"We'll keep that in mind," Jake said.

As Bradley left the tent, Jake turned to Dana and proudly said, "I knew you were a badass, I've never seen you do *that*."

"What can I say? I thrive under pressure," Dana said coolly.

"Well, there might still be a lot more pressure to deal with."

16. Aerial Surveillance

The next morning, Bradley was telling Jake and Dana what processes he and his men had been through so far.

"As you know, we've already searched at the bottom of the waterfall, which obviously proved to be useless, but we searched down there as a starting point," Bradley said.

"And destroyed valued vegetation and natural habitats while doing so," Dana said sourly.

"Yeah, and if you had done your research on Joseph Harrison, you would have known he was leading us somewhere else, otherwise what's the point?" Jake said quickly.

"Hold your horses," Bradley said. "We did realise your point, which is why we're up here now, but I'm a man that likes to cover extra bases, just to be sure."

Jake wasn't entirely convinced, but he moved on quickly because even though he and Dana didn't particularly like Walker and a lot of Bradley's men, Bradley's presence still gave them some reassurance, even if he was incredibly intimidating.

"Anyway," Bradley said. "We're up here now because we have reason to believe the treasure is lying beneath us."

"Yeah we know," Jake said. "*Beneath the quill, beyond the fall of the Sutherland.* What's the plan from here?" he said, eager to get on with the task at hand.

"Well, we want to get underneath the lake, but we can't use explosives on the lake floor due to obvious reasons. We think that the only way Harrison could've got underneath this lake is through some sort of cave system," Bradley said.

"Yes, and we think there might be one literally behind the waterfall and that we'll have to repel down that cliff face to get there," Jake said.

"Before we discuss that, Walker wants a word with both of you."

As Jake and Dana got to Walker's tent, they discovered he was already waiting for them, standing with his arms crossed while his black, slicked back hair and piercing green eyes made his scowl seem even more evil than expected. Jake and Dana really didn't like this guy.

Walker slowly approached them and said, "I don't have much to say to you two *brats*, but I—"

"Ah, I see this conversation has had a civilised start," Jake said interruptedly.

"Shut it," Walker said aggressively. "I know I have to deal with you two looking for the treasure with us, but that's all it is. You even *think* about taking the treasure for yourselves and I'll shoot you myself," he said sternly. "Is that clear?"

"I'm sorry. Dana, did you hear something?" Jake asked cheekily.

"Um, no I don't think so," Dana said, going along with it.

"Unbelievable," Walker said annoyingly. "You don't want to mess with me," he said seriously.

"Yeah, we get your point," Jake said. "Come on, Dana, let's get out of here."

Jake and Dana found Bradley waiting for them outside. He and his men looked set to go.

"So the cave within the cliff face is definitely a possibility, but we've done some aerial surveillance with a couple of our drones and so far we've spotted three more easily accessible cave openings not far from here. We want to search those first to rule out any additional possibilities," Bradley explained.

This time Jake couldn't really argue back. He saw the logic and potential significance in exploring those caves.

"One group will be going to the north-east, Walker and his group will be going south-south-west, and we will be going approximately seven hundred meters north-west of here," Bradley said.

"So, no one is staying behind?" Jake asked.

"No. We're all on the move," Bradley said.

Jake and Dana were satisfied with that.
"Well then, let's get to it," Jake said excitingly.

17. Prevailing Conditions

Even though their trip was quite short and similar to the bike journey up, it still proved to be difficult to navigate. Yet again there were sections of loose gravel and jagged rocks, and Bradley almost had a horrific slip on a steep decline.

With about fifty meters to go, they had to make their way over a large embankment. Once they were over, the cave was in sight. It had a large opening that was about ten meters tall and fifteen wide, and they could see nothing but blackness inside. Despite how ominous it seemed, it was still very secluded due to the coverage provided by the steep embankments and mountain tops surrounding it.

"Before we go in there, can I have a private word with Dana?" Jake asked.

"Sure. We won't go in without you," Bradley said as he and some of his men made their way forward.

Once they were out of earshot, Jake said to Dana, "Listen, I don't know what's ahead of us in this cave. I know you always have my back, but you don't have to come down with me. I'd feel–"

"Jake stop this nonsense. You're never gonna persuade me to go back," Dana said. "Unless you're chickening out? she asked cheekily.

"Shut up," Jake said playfully. "You ready?"

"You know I am," Dana said determinedly.

As they regrouped with Bradley and his men at the entrance of the cave, Bradley said, "Flashlights. We're gonna need them."

Jake and Dana pulled out their flashlights they bought from the hardware store. They had powerful LEDs that emitted a strong beam of light. Even so, they could barely see beyond twenty meters in front of them since there was a vast stretch of darkness in front of them.

They walked down a slow decline for about fifty meters before they spotted anything aside from darkness or rock, then suddenly, a bat flew just above Dana's head.

Dana swiftly ducked. "How rude."

They kept moving and the further they went, the more they discovered. They could hear loud fluttering of wings, something that sounded like rushing water, and they saw strange insects and spiders walking along the edges of rocks and disappearing into crevices.

"Something seems a bit off with those spiders," one of Bradley's men said.

"That's probably because they live in these caves and have very different adaptations compared to spiders that live in outside habitats that humans are more familiar with," Jake said.

"Which textbook did you swallow?" the man said.

Jake simply brushed the joke away since they were all focused on progressing further.

As they continued, the wing fluttering and the sound of rushing water was getting louder. They thought they could see some light up ahead, and as they edged closer, what came into view made them breathless. What they saw were hundreds of bioluminescent stalagmites and stalactites, along with thousands of bats either hanging from the cave ceiling or flying around irritably.

"Wow, this is incredible," Dana said.

"Yeah, not many people get to see bioluminescence on such a huge scale," Jake said, very much impressed.

"Yeah, but we still don't know where that water sound is coming from and I'm sure we're all curious to know, so let's push on," Bradley said.

As they were trying to make their way around the vast mounds of stalagmites on the cave floor, Jake slipped and landed hard on his back, but he was still moving. He was sliding down a steep and slimy embankment. He saw that the embankment ended at a ledge of darkness, so he tried to grab hold of one of the stalagmite mounds, but it broke because of his momentum. He was trying his best to gain any sort of traction, but he couldn't. The last thing he heard before he went tumbling off the edge was Dana screaming his name.

18.   Past Messages

When Jake woke up, he was soaked, and his neck was aching severely. When he sat up he noticed there was a powerful stream of water just in front of him between two walls of rock, but it curved to the right of him and went further downwards. Jake discovered that he was stuck on a rock platform at the turning point of the stream. He figured the momentum he carried must have thrust him onto the rock platform instead of carrying him further down, and he was grateful for it. The last thing he remembered was violently thrashing in the water until he somehow lost consciousness. He noticed a small, dark cave to his left within the wall of rock. He couldn't shout to Dana and Bradley since the water was too loud and he didn't know how far down he was, but he needed to get moving and the small cave was the only option.

Jake had lost his flashlight when he fell, but he came prepared and carried a spare in his backpack. He pulled it out and when he tried to turn it on, it wasn't working. He figured it probably got damaged during the violent trip down.

With a broken flashlight, nowhere to go but the unknown of the smaller dark cave with strange creatures, he could almost see the humour in the situation.

What could go wrong? Jake thought.

Jake slowly edged his way along the cave wall, with his hands and feet carefully feeling for any sort of drastic change in his path. After a painstaking ten minutes, he felt he had made a few turns within the small cave and he suddenly felt an itch on his right hand. He realised something was crawling on it, and it was a giant spider. He swiftly flicked it off and started almost jogging forwards.

Going towards the direction where the spider came from, what a great idea, Jake thought.

After progressing for about another five minutes, he thought he could see a glimmer of light and could hear what sounded like running footsteps as well. He abandoned the wall-edging approach and started running. In a quick dash he reached an intersecting section of cave and he almost crashed into a group of people. It was Dana, Bradley and his men.

"Jake!" Dana shouted as she threw her arms around him. "I'm so glad you're alright."

"What the hell happened to you?" Bradley asked, looking at the state of Jake.

"Had a tough time with the stream back there. Anyway, we're together now," Jake said. "So, what's the plan?" he asked for what felt like the millionth time.

"Well, the plan was to find you, but here we are. Now the plan would be to venture further into this cave, if you're up to it," Bradley said.

"Yeah, let's get moving," Jake said, and he started leading the pack.

They continued walking and didn't discover anything new for a short while. For Jake, the calmful and uneventful few minutes of walking down this cave was very different to what he had just been through, but he was still really eager to come across some sort of clue or indication left by Joseph Harrison, but Jake was starting to have doubts. Just as his frustration was starting to show, they spotted something.

They saw what seemed to be a very bright glimmer of light coming from around a bend. As they made their way past the bend, what they saw was both disappointing and horrifying. Fifty meters in front of them was a cave exit emitting streaks of daylight, but lying right next to them against the wall, was a skeleton.

"What the–" Dana said, surprised.

Next to the skeleton there was a hat covered in mould as well as a very old and faded diary.

"What do we have here?" Jake said in curiosity as he was picking up the diary.

As Jake was flipping through the diary, he discovered that the owner of the diary was named Edward McRae who was a young professor from the

University of Sydney. There was an alarming look on Jake's face as he started reading the last diary entry.

18th of March 1987.

I don't have much time. I've been on the hunt for Harrison's treasure for years. This is the closest I've come to finding it. I think I know where it is, but it's not here. I've purposefully led my pursuers in the wrong direction. It has to be directly behind the waterfall, if not, then my life's research has failed me. I hope someone worthy finds Harrison's treasure. If this bullet wound doesn't finish me off, these snakes sure will.

This is Professor Edward McRae, signing off.

"Brutal," Jake said. "But I have to say that this letter only proves Dana and I right, we need to get back to the waterfall."

"Wait a second," Dana said. "Did that thing say that there are snakes in this cave?"

"Yeah, but they're sure to be long gone by now, this diary entry is thirty years old," Jake said.

"More on the other information," Bradley said. "If there have been other people before us searching for this treasure, we could be in for a huge disappointment. We better get back to that waterfall ASAP."

And suddenly, they heard the deafening sound of infinite hisses. When they turned around, they saw an endless pit of snakes violently slithering their way forward.

"RUN!" Bradley shouted.

They stormed away in the opposite direction towards the light.

As they were running, Dana shouted, "Can't you just shoot them?!"

"We don't have enough ammo!" Bradley shouted back, clearly correct due to the sheer quantity of snakes in pursuit.

They were approaching the cave exit fast, but the ferocious snakes weren't far behind. They only had one option.

Bradley shouted, "JUST JUMP!"

And when they got to the cave exit, they leapt their way out with so much momentum that forced them into an endless sequence of tumbles.

19. Revelations

Luckily the cave they had just explored consistently decreased in altitude, so they didn't have a life-threatening journey of tumbles down to the ground, but that didn't stop them from forming nasty cuts and bruises on their descent.

"Jeez," Dana said, struggling to get up. "That could've gone a lot better."

"Look on the bright side, it could've gone a lot *worse*," Jake said.

"I never get tired of that optimism," Dana said proudly.

"I learn from the best," Jake said, as Dana smiled.

After they caught their breath and brushed off the stones that stuck to them, Bradley said, "According to the aerial surveillance we did earlier, we should be able to loop around to the north of the waterfall and easily make our way back from there."

As they were navigating their way through the shrubbery, Jake asked Bradley, "So, how did you end up working with someone like Walker?"

"Why the sudden interest?" Bradley asked.

"Just trying to satisfy my curiosity," Jake said.

"Ok," Bradley said. "Well, I've spent a large portion of my life in the military, succeeding as a soldier. Two tours in Afghanistan and two in Iraq. Walker was also in the military, but he was a soldier clerk, someone more involved in the paperwork processes, definitely an unprecedented role for someone born with a silver spoon in his mouth. Eventually though, he got tired of tediously serving other people and wanted something big of his own. He ended up pitching his business ideas to myself and different groups of people. I was onboard since he offered more than substantial pay. I've been doing jobs of various scales for him ever since."

"I assume you offered physical, combat-type training for Walker?" Jake asked, remembering the theatrics from the previous day.

"That would be a correct assumption," Bradley said. "It was something he requested after recruiting us."

"Well, it's certainly an interesting story," Jake said.

After hearing that story, Jake and Dana looked at each other in unified mystery, as if to signify to each other that they weren't entirely convinced. The story indicated that Bradley was someone who had honour, someone who was serving the military *for the greater good of society*. Even if Bradley was allured by the prospect of Walker's money, Jake and Dana sensed that Bradley had an ulterior motive. So many questions arose in Jake and Dana's heads. They thought that Dana's dad, Ryan, could not arrive soon enough.

20. After All These Years

As they rose over the final embankment and Lake Quill came into view, they saw that the other two groups had already made it back, looking rather bored due to the lack of activity.

"Took you long enough," Walker said as they approached.

"Yeah, we had some obstacles along the way," Bradley said.

"What happened?" Walker asked.

Bradley explained the story of Jake's mishap, the fiery snakes, the rapid exit and most importantly, the diary discovery.

Walker eyed Jake as if to say it was a pity he made it back alive, but then he said, "I'm glad someone came across something, because all of us came up with nothing."

"Well, there's only one way to go now," Bradley said.

"Beyond the fall of the Sutherland," Jake and Dana said in dramatic unison as Walker rolled his eyes.

It took Bradley's men fifteen minutes to set up all the climbing rope and equipment. As they were finishing up, Bradley came to Jake and Dana and said, "So, we've set up five lines. The lines will be occupied by myself, Walker, you two, and another one of my guys. If we're not back for a considerable amount of time, others will come down and investigate. You ready?"

"You bet we are," Jake said.

The three of them walked alongside the lake to the edge of the cliff by the waterfall. When they got there, a wave of nervousness shook Jake and Dana since they thought the view was even more intimidating than before.

Jake whistled in astonishment. "Five hundred and eighty meters to the bottom. That's a long way down. Bradley, you better have these lines securely anchored."

"Yeah, I've double checked everything, and I'm satisfied with it all," Bradley said encouragingly. "Let's get you hooked up."

"Not without me," a familiar voice said from behind.

As they turned around, they saw it was Ryan, Dana's dad.

Dana went in for a hug and Jake cracked a smile at the sudden feeling of reassurance. But then, there was a quick expression of surprise from both Bradley and Ryan.

"I'll be damned," Bradley said. "Ryan Evans, a man I thought I'd never see again."

"It's certainly unexpected to see you after all these years," Ryan said.

And as they shook hands, something seemed off. Jake looked over at Dana and just knew she was thinking the same thing. There was more to this than it simply being a surprise reunion.

21.   An Unlikely Team Up

After Bradley explained a few details about the current situation to Ryan, Bradley introduced Ryan to Walker. Jake and Dana could sense immediate tension between Ryan and Walker. They were curious to see how this would affect the events they had ahead of them.

"So, are we going down now?" Ryan asked, clearly eager to get on with it, just like his daughter.

"Yeah," Bradley said shortly before informing one of his men that Ryan will be replacing him on the climb down.

"Hang on," Dana said, "How do you two know each other?"

Ryan took a longer moment than usual to respond, as if he meant to hide some key details, and then he simply said, "We used to work together a long time ago."

"What kind of work?" Dana asked.

"That doesn't matter right now," Bradley said quickly. "Let's just get down there, shall we?"

"For sure," Jake said, but he and Dana yet again looked at each other in thoughtful curiosity as they made their way to the climbing lines.

They had to brush off their curiosity quickly since they couldn't afford any distractions on the way down. As they were getting set up, they agreed it was best for

Jake and Dana to climb down together while Ryan would be next to them, separating them from Bradley and Walker. Once they were securely hooked up, Jake looked at Dana and asked, "You ready?"

"Do you even have to ask that anymore?" Dana said positively.

Jake smiled.

"Alright, let's do this," Bradley said. "Just ease into it, step by step. If at any point you feel uncomfortable, feel free to climb back up, or call me or Ryan to assist you. Is that understood?"

"Loud and clear, boss," Dana said to everyone's agreement.

"Ok then," Bradley said.

They slowly started their way down. Each step, and every movement, smooth and precise. The first twenty meters went by slowly, but smoothly. The next ten meters were a little more agonizing due to a small section of sharp outcrops and smoothly worn out surfaces from heavy erosion.

As they climbed further downward, Jake gazed below himself and thought he spotted an opening within the cliff face and said, "Guys, I think I see th—"

But he slipped.

Luckily he was secured on the line and he caught himself steadily.

"You good, Jake?" Ryan asked.

"Yeah...yeah," Jake said, although his heart was racing.

After Jake regained his composure, they resumed their journey downwards. Sure enough, after another twenty meters down, they indeed saw an opening which was getting bigger and bigger.

"It's no wonder you can't see it from the ground. It's completely covered by the water," Dana said.

"Yeah, I'm also starting to wonder how Harrison actually found this cave, but he obviously went to great lengths to store his treasure in crazy places like this," Jake said.

"Damn right about that," Ryan said as they got right next to the cave opening.

"Ok, let's cut the chatter and get in," Walker said impatiently.

The only problem was that the opening was very close to the water and getting hit with the full volume of water at that height could prove dangerous. So they had to squeeze themselves against the cliff and slowly inch their way toward the opening. It wasn't an easy process due to the awkward and uncomfortable nature of each movement, but after a painstaking couple minutes, they all eventually successfully made their way inside.

"That's one long cave," Dana said as they all shone their torches around the cave walls.

The cave seemed to stretch on for what seemed like forever, and it seemed that there wasn't much to it, just endless rock and a vast stretch of darkness ahead.

"Onwards and forwards, I guess," Jake said.

They continued at a steady pace and there didn't seem to be much cause for concern, but they still remained cautious because of the previous incidents Jake, Dana and Bradley had experienced earlier. There wasn't any significant change for the next two hundred meters and that's when Walker started to get annoyed. Bradley was about to say something but then Dana butted in.

"You know, you can't just have everything handed to you, Walker? I doubt Harrison would've placed his treasure in the middle of the cave simply waiting for someone else to come pick it up. He would've gone through severely intricate processes to hide it effectively. So quit your yapping and keep moving," Dana said.

Walker stopped in his tracks and looked very angry.

"What do you think gives *you* the right to preach to *me* and give *me* orders?" Walker said menacingly. "I've just about had it with you and your little boyfriend," he said as he was stepping towards Dana.

"Ok, that's enough," Ryan said as he intervened and firmly placed a hand on Walker's chest, forcing him to back off.

Jake and Ryan weren't exactly happy with Walker's display of attitude towards Dana, but their desire to find the treasure outweighed anything they wanted to do to Walker, so they walked further into the darkness.

After a few minutes of silent and cautious walking, they thought they could see something up ahead. When they got closer, they realised it was a fork in the cave, separating a left path from a right path.

"How are we going to play this?" Bradley asked. "Try one path and if that fails, we try the next one? Or do we split up?"

"I say we split up," Jake said. "That way we can cover more ground in less time."

"I agree," Dana said in unison with Ryan.

"Ok then. I'll take the right path with Walker while you three can take the left path," Bradley said.

"Ok, let's go," Walker said impatiently.

"Not so fast," Jake said.

"What now?" Walker asked irritably.

"We can't risk you finding the treasure and disappearing without us. Dana and I will go with you, while Bradley and Ryan can go together down the other path," Jake said, figuring that was the best option available.

Walker gave Jake a look of deep contempt and annoyance, but he knew that Jake was right, which displeased him even further.

"Fine," Walker said reluctantly, before releasing a heavy sigh.

"Should we agree on a time to get back here?" Dana asked.

"I think we should explore as much as we can and only return back to camp when we have a valid reason to," Ryan said.

"Alright. Let's do this," Jake said, and then the two groups advanced down their separate paths.

22.   History Arises

As Ryan and Bradley were making their way down their cave path and searching for any sort of treasure related clue, Bradley said, "It's been a long time since we've worked together, hasn't it, Ryan?" His voice thick with mystery from the echoes on the cave walls.

"It has," Ryan said. "I never thought I'd see you again, especially after what you did in Montréal."

"What happened in Montréal wasn't my fault. I thought I was doing the right thing," Bradley said.

Ryan stopped in his tracks as if he couldn't believe what he was hearing.

"Doing the right thing? Bradley you went against the code! You went against everything our team stood for!" Ryan said, as heat was rising in his face.

"You'll never understand," Bradley said.

"At least we agree on something then," Ryan said.

"Look, the past is in the past, I—"

"Just stop," Ryan interrupted. "You'll never get my forgiveness for what you did. Let's just find this treasure and then we can go our separate ways."

"That's fine with me," Bradley said.

"Good. But if you ever think about double crossing me, Dana, or Jake, then you'll have serious problems," Ryan said menacingly.

"Funny," Bradley said. "Because I said the same thing to them."

Ryan gave Bradley a threatening look, but he said what he needed to, so he turned and continued to walk, returning his focus to finding treasure.

There was a lot of history behind Ryan and Bradley's relationship that Jake and Dana didn't know about, and Ryan certainly hoped it wouldn't get in the way of them finding this treasure safely.

23. A Troubled Leap

"I'm starting to get sick of these caves," Walker said as they plunged ever deeper into the cave system.

"Although you didn't have to deal with nasty snakes or tumbling down a mountain like us, you've actually just said something that we can agree with," Jake said.

"Well don't get too worried, I'm sure there are many more disagreements to come," Dana said cheekily.

Jake smirked whereas Walker rolled his eyes. "Cut the chatter, blondie. If you talk too much you might get distracted."

Jake came to her defence. "There's about a zero percent chance of Dana losing her concentration. And there's literally just darkness in front of us anyway. Plus, you were the one that initiated this little interaction in the first place."

While Jake and Walker got into another argument, Dana hung back and spotted something of interest on the cave wall.

"Jake..."

There was no response since Jake was now deep in argument with Walker.

"Jake!" Dana said a bit louder.

"What?" Jake said finally.

"Come take a look at this," Dana said.

There was a small circular carving in the wall and within the circle was the familiar design of an anchor with diagonal lines behind it.

Jake gasped. "That's Harrison's sigil!"

"I thought you might recognise it," Dana said.

"This must be Harrison's way of telling us that we're close," Jake said.

"Well then, let's keep going and get even closer," Dana said enthusiastically.

After a few minutes they started to see more changes in the cave. It was no longer just a flat surface. There were a few random rocky formations and small holes in the cave walls that insects kept crawling out of. As they were walking further, something made Jake come to a halt.

"What's wrong?" Dana asked.

"Do you see what I see?" Jake asked.

"No..." Dana said.

"That," Jake said whilst pointing at the floor, "It looks like a scorpion."

"Oh!" Dana said, suddenly concerned.

"Ok, I think it's a good idea to keep going," Walker said.

But as they kept moving, there were more and more scorpions crawling out of the cave walls, each one of them firing nasty hisses that boomed off the walls from the sheer volume.

"This is not good, at all," Jake said, slightly frightened.

The vast quantity of scorpions just kept getting larger until the point where Jake, Dana and Walker were almost completely surrounded.

Dana looked at Jake and shouted, "RUN!"

And the three of them stormed off in the only direction they could go; forward.

"This confuses me!" Jake yelled out while sprinting. "New Zealand is a very isolated country and its ecosystems developed independently over millions of years. There have never been any reported poisonous animals that are lethal. And now we come across deadly snakes *and* scorpions!"

"This isn't the time for your educated facts, Jake. Just keep running!" Dana yelled back.

They were quickly approaching another fork in the cave. The left path had a slight incline whereas the right path had a steep decline.

"Which way?" Dana shouted, almost breathless while their feet were still pounding on the floor.

"Let's go left!" Walker shouted back.

Walker was ahead of them and reached the left path with no problem. But then a whole heap of scorpions quickly appeared out of nowhere, blocking Jake and Dana from accessing the left path and forcing them to take the right.

As Jake and Dana arrived at the right path, they didn't slow down, and they kept sprinting down the steep decline. But they were going too fast and they both slipped and landed on their backs and their momentum carried them into a slide. They looked back and didn't see the scorpions following them, which was a relief, but that relief disappeared very quickly when they turned back around and saw what they were rapidly approaching.

A few meters ahead of them there was a large gap in the cave floor. It would require a very powerful jump to reach the other side successfully. If they didn't make it, they would have to suffer the consequence of taking the brunt of what looked like a ten-meter drop.

As they were sliding nearer the edge, Jake shouted, "Jump on three!"

"One."

"Two."

"Three!"

They launched themselves off the edge into the air and it was as if they were almost frozen in time, precariously looking across the gap they were flying over, not entirely confident of their chances of making it across. And suddenly, they were coming down. Their trajectory was too low for them to land on their feet, and their bodies slammed hard against the edge. Jake managed to latch his hands on to the surface, but Dana didn't have such luck and slipped. As she was falling, Jake grabbed hold of her arm in his left hand. The only reason they hadn't fallen yet was because Jake was holding on for dear life with his right hand, but that too, was slipping.

    Suddenly, the prospect of having to deal with the consequence of taking the brunt of a ten-meter drop seemed very real to them, because Jake couldn't hold on.

24. Mistrust

After the mishap between Bradley and Ryan earlier, they plunged much deeper into the system of caves, looking for any sort of inconsistency that might lead them to the treasure. They had been progressing for close to an hour until they discovered something rather undesirable.

"Well, this sucks," Bradley said in disappointment.

"Yeah it does," Ryan said in agreement. "But it's also good news in a way. We know that the treasure isn't here, which means that Jake, Dana and Walker are probably getting close."

"Or we just missed something and you're completely wrong."

"I highly doubt that," Ryan said. "We searched this place inch by inch. Why do you think it took us so long?"

"I suppose you have a point."

"Well then, let's go find Jake, Dana and Walker."

As Ryan turned around to make his way back, he heard a sound that was far too familiar to him; the cocking of a pistol, which Bradley was now aiming at his head.

"Bradley, what are you doing?" Ryan asked calmly. He had been in worse situations before and he knew that the only way to get out of them was to have a calm and steady focus.

"Do you think I'm just going to let you harvest the rewards of finding this treasure with me?" Bradley asked rhetorically. "No. After what happened when we last saw each other, you can't be trusted."

"Look, I get that you don't like me, and that you don't trust me. The feeling is mutual," Ryan said. "But think about what you're doing. How will you deal with Jake and Dana if they find out, and probably escape?"

Bradley smirked. "They don't need to find out, and they won't have a chance to escape," Bradley said ominously.

Ryan had to think of a way out of this problem, and he had to do it fast.

"Get on your knees," Bradley said.

"Wow, so unoriginal. Why don't you just shoot me and get it over with?" Ryan said, hoping the backchat would buy him some time.

"I don't just want to shoot you, I want to humiliate you."

"If you want me on my knees, you'll have to push me down yourself," Ryan said with conviction.

As Bradley got closer to Ryan, he aimed a kick behind Ryan's knee, but Ryan had anticipated that. Ryan pivoted around in less time than it took for Bradley to blink. He wildly swept Bradley's other foot from under him, which sent the pistol flailing into the air, which Ryan caught, before Bradley landed hard on his back.

"Like I said, you should have just shot me and got it over with," Ryan said.

Bradley's face flushed with anger. He sprung up to his feet and charged at Ryan. He aimed a powerful punch towards Ryan's face, but Ryan quickly sidestepped and launched an uppercut, rapidly connecting the butt of the pistol to Bradley's chin. Bradley was unconscious before he hit the ground.

Unsure of how long Bradley would be unconscious for, Ryan started sprinting in the opposite direction.

25. A Thought Of Possibilities

Walker was wandering amongst the cave system, tediously going over the same observation processes he had been doing for the last few hours. Walker felt a familiar wave of annoyance take over him because he had been in this cave system for hours and still hadn't come up with anything, but he was also worried. After Jake and Dana were forcibly separated from him a few moments earlier, he started wondering if there was a chance that the two of them could secretly find the treasure and double cross him. But he wasn't going to let that happen, because he knew that there was an equal possibility of the treasure lying on the very path he was walking on. So he pressed on, determined to finally get what he came for.

26. Advice

It wasn't the first time Jake woke up with a throbbing headache, and he knew it wouldn't be the last time either. He lay on the floor for a moment, reflecting on what just happened and how lucky he and Dana were to come away from the fall with just a couple scrapes.

"That...was scary," Dana said as she was sitting up, almost breathlessly.

"Yeah. If we hadn't landed on our sides with our entire bodies absorbing the impact, the outcome would've been much worse," Jake said.

"We'll need to thank my dad for that tip later," Dana said.

"For sure," Jake said. "It's amazing that he told us that a few years ago and after all that time it ended up proving useful."

"His advice has a way of being useful in the most unique types of situations."

"Sounds familiar," Jake said, giving Dana a friendly nod.

Dana smiled. "Yeah. My advice is always useful."

"That's debatable," Jake said jokingly.

Dana chuckled. "If I had more energy I would slap you."

"No doubt about that. But it's time to get your energy back. We've still got a treasure to find," Jake said as he stood up.

"Oh yeah, I forgot about that," Dana said sarcastically.

It was Jake's turn to chuckle. "Anyway, we've got two options. The first one is to try and climb this wall and continue down the path we were headed, or we can find another way."

"It's too high to climb. We could end up falling again. I say we find another way," Dana said.

"As usual, I agree. Just like I said earlier, onwards and forwards," Jake said as he held out his hand to assist Dana with standing up.

As Jake helped Dana up, Dana threw her arms around Jake in an affectionate hug.

"That was a close one," Dana said. "We need to be more careful. I don't want you to get hurt."

Jake smiled. "I won't get hurt, and you won't either. Now let's go find this treasure."

27. An Unexpected Instalment

Walker was moving faster and more determined than ever. The longer he went on, the more efficient he got at searching the floor and the walls with his flashlight for something that seemed incongruent relative to the surroundings. He was getting consumed by the process, delving ever deeper into the cave system, until he came to a larger opening in the cave and finally saw something. As he walked into the opening, what he saw was a large, circular space that almost seemed unnatural. At the opposite side of the circular space was where the cave ended, which would have disappointed Walker, but he saw something else as well. Something so out of place that it didn't make sense to him. A glimmer, or some sort of reflection subtly bouncing off the cave walls.

Drawn to the reflection, he stepped forward, but when he planted his foot down on the floor, something moved. It was almost like stepping on a loose brick. And suddenly, he heard a sharp noise behind him. As he turned around, he saw a gigantic and sharp metal blade, rapidly shoot up from the floor all the way to the cave ceiling, completely blocking the exit from where he just came from. He angrily dashed to the other side to see what was causing the reflection, but suddenly, there was no reflection anymore.

"It can't be," he said out loud to himself.

Walker thought it must have been a cleverly engineered illusion, to lure him into this space, where he was trapped, with no way out.

28. A Natural Inconsistency

"Remember when we were little kids and we used to play hide and seek?" Dana asked.

"Yeah, why?" Jake said.

"We used to hide in the most ridiculous places, like that one time I climbed up into my chimney and braced myself on the side walls, or when you lay amongst the vegetation in my back yard and covered yourself with dirt for camouflage," Dana said. "We both used to have such an incredibly difficult time finding each other because we were so playfully competitive. It's like we're playing hide and seek all over again, except we're both seeking for Joseph Harrison's treasure, which is even harder to find."

"That's definitely an interesting take on our situation, but I completely agree," Jake said. "Speaking of seeking, we're also seeking for another way out, because there is no way we can go back the way we came."

"One problem at a time," Dana said, giving Jake a friendly pat on the shoulder.

After a small while of more walking, they spotted something unusual amongst the cave wall. Instead of being solid rock like the rest of the cave, this particular section of the cave wall rather consisted of smaller rocks compressed together, like layers of bricks. It was a natural inconsistency, and it intrigued Jake and Dana.

"Why on Earth is that section different to the rest of the cave?" Jake asked in curiosity.

"I have no idea," Dana said. "Let's take a closer look."

As Dana got closer, she stepped on something, or rather, *in* something.

"Wait a second," Dana said as she frantically looked below her. "Quicksand, I'm standing in quicksand."

"How did we not notice that?" Jake asked, totally not fazed by Dana's situation.

"I don't know, just help me out before I sink," Dana said hurriedly as she was sinking with surprising pace.

"Right. Good idea," Jake said, only half-jokingly.

Jake had to carefully step around the perimeter of the quicksand in order to not meet the same fate as Dana. The closest he could get to her was right up against the cave wall with the compressed rocks.

"Ok, I can't reach, but don't worry, I've got an idea," Jake said. "Take off your backpack and try to get it as close to me as possible."

Dana did as she was told, and Jake could just about reach the tightening straps at the bottom of the bag.

"In order to pull you, I have to pull the bag, so hold on tight," Jake said.

"Ok, go for it," Dana said, whilst her body was getting more and more submerged.

Jake started pulling and it was more difficult than he had anticipated because the quicksand was weighing Dana down. But Jake was still confident. He pulled with all his might and sure enough, he was slowly but surely dragging Dana out of the quicksand.

As Dana was nearly completely out of the quicksand, Jake overcommitted, and he pulled too hard. Such force ejected Dana out of the quicksand, sending her crashing into Jake, and they both smashed through the wall of compressed rocks.

29. Race Against Time

Ryan made it back to the fork in the cave where the group had split up initially, but it had already been several minutes since the tussle between Ryan and Bradley. Ryan knew that he had to find Jake and Dana, and fast.

He started rapidly sprinting down the part of the cave that he knew would take him closer to Jake and Dana, but up until this point, Ryan hadn't thought about Walker. Walker would certainly be an issue since he would sense immediate suspicion by noticing the absence of Bradley.

I'll cross that bridge when I come to it, Ryan thought.

His top priority at the moment, was first finding Jake and Dana.

As he was accelerating down the cave at quite a daring pace, he started to notice some rocky formations and small holes in the cave walls, and random clusters of insects, but still no sign of Jake or Dana.

Suddenly, he came to another fork in the cave, one path on a slight incline to the left, and the other on a steep decline to the right. He stopped momentarily to think about which way to go. The wrong decision could leave Bradley enough time to wake up and possibly get to Jake and Dana before he did.

Ryan thought that Walker, Jake and Dana couldn't have split up due to concerns of trust, so he assumed that they also had to make the choice of left or right. Finally, Ryan came to a decision and chose the path on the right because it seemed like the more challenging option, and therefore, the more logical option due to the challenging nature of their treasure hunting task at hand.

He quickly got moving again, but he had to slow down because he realised the decline didn't last for very long and soon came to a drop of about ten meters in depth. He was about to attempt to jump over to the rock platform on the other side, but something in his mind told him to stop.

I bet Harrison wants us to think that we need to jump over there, to lead us in the wrong direction, Ryan thought.

If Ryan was wrong, he wouldn't be able to get back up and Bradley would get to Jake and Dana first, but if he was right, he would be getting closer to the treasure, and hopefully closer to Jake and Dana. Ryan had to trust himself.

"Here goes nothing," Ryan said out loud, mentally preparing to take the brunt of a ten-meter drop.

And he jumped.

30.   Something Historical

Jake and Dana woke in a heap on the floor with several rocks weighing them down. Jake landed face up and the rocks that were weighing him down were just light enough to move, but when he looked to his left, he saw that Dana was face down and therefore, had difficulty moving.

Jake's left hand was trapped but his right arm was free, so he slowly began rolling off the most easily accessible rocks and eventually, he lightened the load enough to allow himself to forcefully stand up. He then moved to lift the other rocks off Dana's back. This time it was a lot quicker since both of his arms were free. As he lifted off the last rock, he then moved to help Dana to her feet.

"Thanks, Jake," Dana said with a sigh of exhaustion.

"You know, I think if either one of us tried this adventure alone, we wouldn't have made it this far," Jake said.

"If that's not the truth, then I don't know what is," Dana said.

Then as they turned around to explore yet another linkage of the cave system they had found themselves in, what they saw shocked them. They had been so concentrated on each other and getting free from the rocks that they didn't see what was right in front of them.

"Oh. My. Goodness," Jake said in amazement, while Dana's excitement was visually growing too.

What they were staring at was an immaculate wooden stand that spiralled from bottom to top, and perched on top was a ring, the most beautiful ring Jake or Dana had ever seen, silver and encrusted with diamonds and red zircons.

It was if Jake and Dana were in a trance, momentarily unable to effectively form a solid sentence in their head.

Finally, Dana said, "This has got to be it, right? A piece of Joseph Harrison's treasure?"

"That's not just any piece of Harrison's treasure," Jake said. "That is the *Ring of Valour,* which he stole from a very highly guarded facility on the west coast of South Africa in 1928, the second incredible and unthinkable act of what we know was part of *The Heists of Opulence.*"

Jake gulped, but he and Dana finally stepped forward to take a closer look.

"Wow, it's so beautiful that I don't even want to touch it," Dana said.

"Me neither," Jake said in agreement as he was circling the wooden stand that the ring was resting on.

"I wonder what this is," Jake said as he spotted a piece of rolled up parchment behind the wooden stand.

But before Jake and Dana could pick it up and unroll it, they could hear footsteps in the cave, approaching at speed.

31.   A Way Out

Jake and Dana's curiosity led them to investigate who, or what, was trampling down the cave system. They took a peek outside what was now a large open hole which used to be the wall of compressed rocks, and they still had to be careful in order to not stumble into the quicksand laying outside. To their surprise, they saw Ryan storming in their direction.

"There you are," Ryan said, relieved to have found the two of them at last.

"Wait, stop!" Jake said, pointing at the floor as Ryan was approaching them.

Ryan looked down and was surprised by the apparency of the quicksand. "Jeez, that is extremely well camouflaged," he said, panting slightly.

"Yeah, one of us found out the hard way," Dana said.

"What happened to you two? And where is Walker?" Ryan asked.

"Long story short, we were chased by a bunch of scorpions and we were forced to separate from Walker, and then found ourselves here," Jake said.

"It seems like you two have had an eventful time," Ryan said reflectively, observing the pile of rocks behind them. "Anyway, we have to go, now. I had a tussle with Bradley, and he won't take it easy if he finds us."

"Ok, but then we'll need to find a new way out because we can't go back the way we came and we'll need to take this with us," Dana said.

"Take what with us?" Ryan asked with a sudden increase of interest.

Jake and Dana moved away from each other so Ryan could have a proper look at the space they were standing in, giving him a clear view of the *Ring of Valour*.

"Holy..." Ryan said, almost speechless.

"That was pretty much our reaction," Jake said.

"Ok," Ryan said, regaining his composure. "Let's grab it and get out of here."

Jake looked at Dana and said, "Do you want to do the honours, or shall I?"

"You do it," Dana said. "You're the one that's obsessed with Joseph Harrison, so you deserve it."

"Well, without you we wouldn't even be here," Jake said.

"Just take it, Jake," Dana said, smiling.

"Ok," Jake said, followed by a deep breath.

He slowly grabbed hold of the ring, careful not to knock the stand over or drop the ring in the process. Aside from its extraordinary appearance, Jake realised it didn't feel like a standard ring either. It felt dense, and *powerful*.

He carefully placed it in a tightly zipped compartment in his backpack where he felt it would be most secure.

"Alright," Jake said, letting out a deep breath. "Let's go."

"Wait. Where do you suppose this goes?" Dana asked, pointing at a small trickle of water heading down a narrow pathway up against the cave wall, which they hadn't noticed earlier.

"It could be a way out," Ryan said. "But we need to make a decision. We either go back and head further down the other part of the cave system, or down here. But quite frankly, I vote for this way because I'm sick of those caves behind us."

"Agreed," Jake and Dana said simultaneously.

"Alright then," Ryan said. "Let's get to it."

"But we can't forget this," Dana said, picking up the piece of rolled up parchment behind the wooden stand, before following the path of trickled water.

32.   An Undiscovered Exit

Much of the narrow pathway Jake, Dana and Ryan were travelling down was very similar to the rest of the cave system they had already explored; with vast amounts of darkness between what seemed like endless stretches of rock.

Jake and Dana updated Ryan on everything that happened, and Ryan did the same for them.

"So, let me get this straight," Jake said. "Bradley pulled a gun on you because he doesn't trust you due to whatever happened in Montréal way back when. Is that correct?"

"Yes," Ryan said.

"And what exactly happened between you two in Montréal?" Dana asked. "Why were you two even working together in the first place?"

"Unfortunately, that's classified," Ryan said.

"Dad, you go against many police guidelines to tell me information about certain things you do on the job, but now all of a sudden you can't discuss this matter which is obviously more important than ever. Why is that?" Dana asked.

"Look," Ryan said, stopping in his tracks, while Jake slowly walked ahead. "When I say classified, I mean that it's strictly high-government-level classified. So, legally, I'm *really* not allowed to tell you. But maybe

I'll tell you at some point, just not now, or any time soon," he said, hinting that it was the end of the conversation.

"Alright," Dana said. "I get it."

"Hey Dana, Ryan, come over here and check this out," Jake shouted from up ahead.

Dana and Ryan did as they were told and what they saw was that on their left, the cave wall suddenly disappeared and there was also a small drop, mostly filled by a pool of water which was sourced by the trickle of water they were following. They were almost mesmerised by the colour of the water, which was a very bright and almost ultra-coloured blue.

"This cave system is really full of surprises," Jake said.

"Can't deny that," Dana said.

"If my attitude and the circumstances were different and more...pleasant, I would consider jumping in due to the possibility of even more discoveries beneath, but I think we should continue moving," Jake said, observing that the path had started to incline, which was a positive sign since they needed to get closer to the surface.

Unsurprisingly, they had a unanimous agreement, so they continued, on an ascent that felt like it would take forever, until they finally saw something.

"I think I see some light up ahead," Jake said, so they all increased their pace because of the encouraging sign.

As they were getting closer to the top and in turn, the light, Dana said, "At last, an exit."

"Yes, but one we certainly didn't know about," Jake said, observing the shrubbery that was covering the exit. "I guess Bradley's aerial surveillance wasn't fully effective after all."

"Lucky for us," Ryan said. "Let's see where it opens up."

Once they pushed their way past the shrubbery, they realised they were just underneath the crest of a mountain, looking at another impressive view of mountain skyline, high altitude snow, and greenery as far as the eye can see. But when they turned to peek over the crest, they realised they were just behind the crater of Lake Quill.

Ryan made a quick observation of Bradley's camp and said, "Well then, it looks like Bradley and Walker aren't back, and the rest of the camp is completely clueless. The odds are in our favour."

"Then let's get our bikes and get the hell out of here," Dana said.

33. A Second Message

Jake, Dana and Ryan had easily managed to get to their bikes, all they had to do was creep along the outside of the crater around Lake Quill, so they wouldn't be seen by anyone happening to be gazing in the distance from Bradley's campsite. However, since there were two bikes, two of them had to share a bike and there wasn't any space on Ryan's bike due to his bulky physique. Jake and Dana played *rock-paper-scissors* to determine who got to ride the bike and who sat on the back, and the game was in Dana's favour. They only started the bikes at the bottom of the hill to avoid being discovered by any noise disturbance, and from then they made quick work on their journey back to Glenorchy.

"Gosh, that sucked," Jake complained. Sitting on the back of a motorbike on bumpy terrain for a couple hours wasn't the most pleasant experience ever, but he was still happy to be out of harm's way, *for now*.

"Suck it up, buttercup," Dana replied cheekily as she strolled past towards the lake house.

Jake chuckled. He could never get tired of the banter that always existed between them.

"You guys went quite big on the accommodation," Ryan said, admiring the lake house and its serene view. "It's too bad we can't use it much since we're on the clock."

"If we had known what our situation would've turned out to be like this, we would have obviously chosen something cheaper," Jake said as they were stepping inside, which brought a nod of approval from Ryan.

"As much as we'd like to stay here and admire the beauty of this location, you said it yourself, Dad, we're on the clock. Bradley, Walker and their crew could come to their senses any minute," Dana said. "So, Jake, do the honours and unroll the scroll."

"Yes ma'am," Jake said friendly.

As Jake unrolled the scroll of parchment neatly on the table, allowing them all to read it clearly, what was revealed was old-fashioned, ink-written hand writing, which almost looked like it was in cursive, yet still very similar to the engraving on the original concrete slab. The writing appeared to be another one of Joseph Harrison's riddles.

At last upon the second step
reaching west, closer to meridian
amidst the famous cape
within the depths of unconquered
my fortune awaits.

"What on Earth does that mean?" Jake asked.

"Let's quickly figure it out," Dana said. "The first line is not important; he's just telling us that we're onto the next stage. The last line is his famous motto, so the clue lies within the middle three lines."

"Ok," Jake said. "Well, the second line is kind of obvious. We need to be going west and closer to the Greenwich Meridian, but from where we are now that could mean Asia, Europe, Africa or even back to Australia," he said factually.

"I agree," Dana said. "But the third and fourth lines are completely bewildering to me."

Jake and Dana stopped momentarily to think. It wasn't as if they could go to a state library and do some research like last time, this time they were under timely pressure.

And suddenly, Ryan turned around to observe the view, and laughed, quite triumphantly, as if he just thought of the most intelligent idea ever.

"What's so funny?" Dana asked.

Ryan turned back around, with a smug look on his face and said, "I know where we need to go."

"Ok. Go on then, if you're such a genius," Dana said, almost annoyed by her father's smugness.

"Alright," Ryan said. "We *do* need to go west and closer to the Greenwich Meridian," repeating what Jake and Dana had agreed upon moments ago. "As for the second and third lines, I think that 'famous cape,' is referring to Cape Town, and I think that 'within the depths of unconquered,' is referring to the well-known shipwreck of HMS Invictus, since that shipwreck is indeed located off the coast of Cape Town."

"Wait," Jake said. "Why would 'unconquered' be referring to the HMS Invictus?"

"Because the word 'Invictus,' means 'unconquered,' in Latin," Ryan said confidently.

"Well, well, well, maybe you are a genius after all," Dana said proudly.

"I am deputy chief of police for a reason, you know?" Ryan said.

"Yeah, sure," Dana said cheekily.

"Anyway," Jake said. "It's time to go to Cape Town."

34. Turbulence

"Here we go again," Jake complained, as they were walking on the skybridge into the plane at Auckland Airport.

Jake was more than a little annoyed. He thought he handled the short flight from Glenorchy to Auckland well enough, but the next portion of the trip, according to Jake, was going to be a nightmare. First they needed to fly from Auckland to Sydney, then from Sydney to Johannesburg, and finally, a layover to Cape Town.

"Who on Earth would want to be in a plane for that long?" Jake said.

Dana sighed. "Because, Jake," she said, friendly grabbing his shoulder. "We've got places to be and treasure to find," she said in an exaggerated tone.

Jake eyed her and smiled. "Let's get this show on the road then," he said, with a faked sense of excitement.

The journey wasn't as bad as Jake thought it would be. Sure, there were several moments of turbulence that made him grasp Dana's arm, which always earned him a slap in return, but he made good use of the entertainment available to him.

He managed to watch all the variations of *'Lara Croft,'* and he ended it off with *'The Adventures of*

Tintin,' clearly enthusiastic about keeping on the theme of treasure hunting.

At last, they were coming in for a landing in Cape Town. He didn't know what day it was because of the confusing nature of the time zones and how long they had been flying, but he guessed it must have been quite late at night. Overall, he was just glad to be on the ground.

"Ok, so I have a friend that stays in a place which isn't far from here. He wasn't happy about the short notice, but he's willing to accommodate us," Ryan explained.

After they paid for the rental car, they noticed, coincidentally, that it was another Mitsubishi Lancer.

"Wow," Jake said. "What are the chances?"

"Slim to none," Dana said factually.

The GPS calculated the drive to be approximately twenty-five minutes, but it was taking longer due to the lack of familiarity.

"Not far now," Dana said, observing that the GPS said that they only had three kilometers to go, thinking about the relief she would feel when she reached the proper comfort of a bed, or a couch.

But suddenly, that thought was disrupted. Ryan had to slam on brakes because there was a car that appeared out of nowhere, almost blocking the entire width of the road. Three men with black clothing and masked hoods came running towards their car, with pistols aimed at the windshield.

"Get out of the car in five seconds or we'll blow your brains out!" one of them shouted violently.

Jake, Dana and Ryan barely had any time to react to what just happened, so they had no choice.

They slowly stepped out of the car with their arms raised and hands in the air. Two of the hooded men circled the car so they were behind Jake and Dana, while the other one stayed at the front, aiming his pistol at Ryan.

"Look, we don't want any harm," Ryan said carefully. "We'll give you what you need."

"Open the trunk," one of them said, gesturing his pistol towards the back of the car.

"Ok," Ryan said as he used the car key to automatically open the trunk.

One of the other men grabbed all of the backpacks, including the one that held the *Ring of Valour*. If Jake's heart hadn't felt like it had dropped to the floor, it sure did now.

Jake didn't know what kind of courage or stupidity was building up inside him, but he couldn't let these thieves get away with their luggage and especially, the *Ring of Valour*.

He suddenly lunged towards the thief manoeuvring the backpacks, but Jake was too slow, and he felt the butt of a pistol connect with his head.

35. Guardian Angel

As Jake woke up his vision was momentarily blurred, but as his senses stabilised, he tried to orientate himself and figure out where he was. What he saw was definitely not what he expected.

He was lying on a couch in what seemed to be a rather upper-class apartment with modern features and to his right, sun was streaking through a glass balcony door that led way to a mesmerising ocean view of Cape Town. As he looked to his left, he saw a woman, and it wasn't Dana. This woman had long, striking black hair and was sitting with her back to Jake, sipping on a cup of black coffee.

"Oh look, he's awake," the woman said, without turning around.

"Where am I? Where are my friends?" Jake asked, now sitting up to prepare for what was probably going to be a very serious conversation.

"Dana and Ryan are just fine. They're sleeping in my guest bedroom."

"How do you know their names?"

"Because I'm the guardian angel who swooped in and rescued you in the nick of time, *Jake*," the woman said, now turning around to face him.

Jake discovered that the rest of her appearance was even more striking, with an unblemished facial structure and intense green eyes.

Jake gulped.

"Wow," Jake said. "What exactly happened?"

"Last night I happened to be driving and saw some civilians in trouble. One of them, you, were on the ground while the other two, Dana and Ryan, had pistols pointed at their heads by three hooded men. Me being me, I instantly hit the brakes, jumped out the door, and shot two of them in the kneecaps. Ryan managed the rest of it since his police training kicked in."

Jake almost didn't know what to say.

"And why are we here?" Jake finally asked.

"Because this is safer than the neighbourhood you were originally heading to."

"Well, thank you," Jake said, with sincerity in his voice.

"Yeah, whatever," the woman said carelessly. "But you better think twice before you do something stupid like that again. You are in South Africa after all, one of the most dangerous countries in the world."

"I'll keep that in mind," Jake said.

The woman got up and started walking towards an intersecting passage.

"Where are you going?" Jake asked.

"To wake your friends. We have important things to discuss."

"Wait," Jake said. "What's your name?"

The woman turned around. "Josephine," she said.

36. Someone New

After Josephine went to wake Dana and Ryan, Dana came to Jake and immediately initiated into a very daunting conversation, which Jake knew was coming, since what he did the night before was extremely dangerous.

"I get that sometimes we need to do crazy things to avoid dangers in the environment, or even to evade Walker like back in New Zealand, but if you ever do something reckless like that again that jeopardises our safety like *that*, I'm done. I mean it," Dana said.

There were no excuses or apologies that could fix what he had done. They were simply lucky that Josephine had come to their rescue.

Jake grabbed Dana's hand and looked her in the eye. "It won't happen again, I promise," he said.

"I know," Dana said. And they hugged.

When they broke apart, Jake suddenly remembered why Josephine woke them in the first place.

"So, what's so important that we need to discuss?" Jake asked.

"Look, Jake," Ryan said. "After Josephine rescued us last night, she asked us why we were here, and we felt compelled to tell her the truth. Josephine wants to help us, and I think it's only fair to accept her offer of help and let her join us. Plus, we could use some local knowledge."

Jake normally would have been discouraged if there were any newcomers trying to stick their noses in, but given the current circumstances, he actually *wanted* Josephine with them.

Jake looked at Josephine and almost gulped again because of her intimidating presence.

But then he jokingly said, "Well, Josephine, welcome to the fiercest treasure hunting group you've ever seen."

Josephine laughed.

"So, where to now?" Jake asked.

"Well, last night Dana and Ryan told me that you're looking for the HMS Invictus. I know exactly where that is," Josephine said.

"Where is it?" Dana asked.

"Just off the coast of the Cape of Good Hope," Josephine said.

"What's the Cape of Good Hope?" Jake and Dana asked in unison.

Josephine chuckled. "Yeah, you're clearly not from around here," she said, smirking at the two of them. "Anyway, let's go. We're burning daylight."

37. The Cape Of Good Hope

Jake, Dana, Ryan and Josephine were strolling along the streets of Cape Town heading towards a storage facility to pick up some scuba gear that Josephine owned, since their own scuba gear was back in Sydney. It was really such a picturesque city and one of the most beautiful cities Jake and Dana had ever seen, with impressive mountain ranges, intense blue ocean views, and a city life that was very aesthetically pleasing.

"Josephine, weren't you saying that this is one of the most dangerous places in the world?" Jake asked as they followed Josephine.

"I said *South Africa* was one of the most dangerous places in the world. In the right places, in the daylight, Cape Town is lovely. It's at night when your problems start, as you witnessed not even twenty-four hours ago," Josephine said.

Jake and Dana were reassured by this, whereas Ryan wasn't particularly concerned at all since he was trained to deal with tricky situations and had a mysteriously dangerous past to prove that.

When they arrived at the storage facility and picked up the various sets of scuba gear Josephine randomly had, Jake asked, "What is it exactly that you do for a living?"

"I'm a university lecturer for the University of Cape Town," Josephine said.

"What do you teach?" Dana asked.

"Marine biology, which is why I have all this," Josephine said, gesturing at all the scuba equipment. "But I'm also qualified to fill in for Legal Studies, and I sometimes run self-defence classes on the weekends."

Jake wasn't exactly surprised by the self-defence classes because of Josephine's incredibly athletic figure, but he was surprised by the fact that Josephine was a university lecturer, because she looked incredibly young and not much older than Jake or Dana.

"Anyway, I have some extra wetsuits for you to wear, but Ryan, we'll definitely have to get a new one for you," Josephine said factually since Ryan was far bulkier than any of them.

"I hope we can find a wetsuit that actually fits me," Ryan said, which the others found funny.

After they fitted the scuba gear into Josephine's rather immense black Ford Raptor, they managed to find Ryan a wetsuit, and they bought some water and snacks to sustain themselves on the hour and a half drive up to the Cape of Good Hope, and for the fact that they didn't know how long they would be there for.

On the drive there, Jake, Dana and Ryan learnt that Josephine had a rough childhood where she had a falling-out with her parents and had a few life-threatening incidents with local thugs. But she clearly made a name for herself and was now someone that was well respected, but also feared by many members of the local community.

If that's not an inspiration to live by, I don't know what is, Jake thought.

As they arrived at the Cape of Good Hope, what they saw was land that converged into a rocky cliff that projected beyond any other point they looked at. There were also a couple beaches either side of the cliff, and toward the horizon, was ocean water as far as the eye can see. They truly felt like they were at the end of the Earth.

"Wow, this is incredible," Dana said.

"Coming from Australia, I thought you would be used to this kind of scenery," Josephine said.

"Well, we are, but this is still seriously impressive nonetheless," Dana said.

"I'm glad you can appreciate what this place has to offer," Josephine said, before she started walking towards the beach.

"Hang on, I just realised something," Jake said.

"What's that?" Dana asked.

"The reason Joseph Harrison chose the HMS Invictus for this next clue, was because his father was the captain of that ship. I knew I recognised that name from somewhere," Jake said.

"Wow," Dana said. "Pretty crazy way to honour his father."

"I know," Jake said. "Now let's go find Harrison Senior's shipwreck."

38.   HMS Invictus

Once they made their way down to the beach and all fitted themselves with the oxygen tanks, much needed flashlights and carried out the usual safety checks, they swam toward the famous shipwreck. Josephine claimed to have observed it briefly once before, so she knew that it was only about one hundred meters from the shoreline, which was luckily still in a relatively shallow area that could be accessible by swimming. Even with the weight of oxygen tanks, that distance with fitted swimming flippers was no challenge at all. They agreed to came back for the dinghy on the back of the Ford Raptor if they really needed it.

They had only been swimming for a few minutes before Josephine said that they were now in the general vicinity of the shipwreck. As they swam downward, their ears had to adjust to the change in pressure, but all four of them had some sort of diving experience so they weren't too concerned. It didn't take them long to spot the massive shipwreck lying on the sea floor. Apart from the lack of a full hull, a few holes on the side, the expansive growth of algae and the occasional fish swimming in and out of the ship, it was surprisingly intact for a ship that had been sunk for one hundred years, and quite a spectacle to look at.

Jake and Dana simultaneously stopped and looked at each other, as if to express their amazement to each other. Then Dana pointed downward, signalling that she was eager to get inside, so they all followed suit.

Once they got inside, they weren't surprised to see that the ship was practically empty. All they could see was the sand of the sea floor, more algae, and wooden panels providing the remaining support of the ship. But they knew that there was still a chance of finding something if they kept looking.

So they split up and searched the entire ship, or at least what was left it. They looked everywhere; behind some of the wooden panels, on the roof of the ship, Ryan went to have a look on top of the ship, and they all even dug up some of the sand to test their luck in that area. After all that, Josephine looked at Jake and pointed at the oxygen tanks and made a cut-throat gesture with her hands, as if to warn him about oxygen depletion.

But then Jake spotted something. Just behind a layer of algae, he saw a slight engraving on one of the horizontal wooden panels that they missed. Jake quickly wiped away the algae and then saw the familiar design of an anchor with diagonal lines behind it; Joseph Harrison's sigil. He then saw that there were holes on each side of the panel, acting as what he assumed were handles. He tried pulling the panel out, but it was too heavy, so he rapidly motioned Ryan over for an assist. But before Ryan made it over there, Josephine shoved Jake out of the way and much to Jake's surprise, she yanked out the panel with such strength that Jake couldn't quite comprehend.

As Josephine pulled out the panel, they noticed it extended into a larger, rectangular box, which would explain the weight. And there was a final engraving on the top.

Within the famous sound of the city, seen from the light of Robben.

They quickly memorised it and then pointed upwards, signalling it was time to surface, because they really needed to, and fast. They swam as fast as they could, kicking wildly and getting a tremendous amount of help from their flippers. They were getting so close, but then, around twenty meters from the surface, Dana run out of oxygen. But she wasn't fazed, and rapidly continued swimming upwards with the others, and they all managed to take a breath of fresh air when they resurfaced.

"So, a short riddle this time," Dana said. "I wonder what it means."

"I know what it means," Josephine said.

39. Consequences

"What does it mean?" Dana asked as they began swimming back towards the beach.

"Well, I can't tell you exactly what the first half means, but the second half is definitely referring to the lighthouse on Robben Island. Once we get there, I'm sure we will figure out where the first half of the riddle is pointing us to," Josephine said.

"Interesting choice of venue, I wonder what made him choose it," Ryan said.

"Maybe it provides a unique viewpoint that no other place does, hopefully giving away the next location," Dana said, earning a nod of approval from Jake.

"How far away is that?" Jake asked.

"We just need to get to a ferry terminal near central Cape Town, which is pretty much where we just came from, so an hour and a half worth of driving" Josephine said.

"Let's head there right away then, but let's drop all of this stuff off first since it sounds like we don't need it," Ryan said.

"Roger that," Jake said, before they sped up, eager to start the journey toward the next clue.

As they got to the beach, they sprinted up the stairs towards where the Ford Raptor was parked. When they reached the top, they could see the monstrosity of a vehicle slightly obscured behind a bush, and when they got past the bush, Jake heard the cocking of a pistol. As he looked to his left, he saw the pistol aimed at his head, and the person holding the pistol was Bradley. Next to Bradley and looking very smug, was Walker.

"Well, well, well, look what the cat dragged in," Walker said with evil undertones.

"How on Earth did you find us?" Jake asked, anger rising inside him.

"I have my ways," Walker said.

Jake was getting even angrier now. He had to fight the urge to absolutely climb into Bradley or Walker. He didn't want to do anything stupid that would put the other three in harm's way.

But Bradley edged closer to Jake and said, "I told you that I wouldn't take it easy on you if you retaliated."

And then Bradley rapidly knocked everyone unconscious, except for Jake.

"It's time for us to have a little talk," Walker said.

40. Change Of Plans

A couple minutes later, Bradley restrained them all and threw them into the back of some sort of SUV, which was smaller than Josephine's Raptor. Jake had to squeeze next to their unconscious bodies and Bradley nearly slammed the door in his face. Walker had a smug expression on his face in the passenger seat.

"You know there was really no need to hit them unconscious, right? If anything, it created more of a hassle for you," Jake said.

"I know, I just felt like it," Bradley said, much to Jake's displeasure.

"So how did you do it then? Did you use a tracker?" Jake asked.

"Oh, to find you?" Walker asked casually.

"Obviously," Jake said, unable to find comfort on the cramped back seats.

"Let's just say, once again, that I have my ways," Walker said, so it still remained a mystery to Jake. "Now, onto the topic at hand," he said, aiming a pistol at unconscious Dana. "You're going to tell me where the next treasure is, or I'm going to blow her brains out."

"How about you go down to the shipwreck and find out yourself?" Jake said defiantly.

"Watch your mouth," Walker said, cocking the pistol nonchalantly.

"Ok, relax," Jake said. "How about we show you?"

Walker thought about that for a moment, and then he said, "I'll accept. But if you try any more antics, you know the consequences," his eyes following the direction of the pistol on Dana. "Now, where are we off to next?"

"We'll lead you there, so you can't just take the information and dump us somewhere that's inaccessible to society," Jake said.

Walker let out an evil laugh. "Very clever," he said. "Now we wait."

41. Robben Island

After they were driving for another hour, they parked in a back street in the outskirts of the city. Josephine was awake first, then Dana and Ryan finally came around. Jake explained the situation to them and that they had to work with Walker and Bradley, *again*.

"So, what now?" Dana asked.

"We get out of these wetsuits and into normal clothes as planned, and then catch a ferry to Robben Island. Only this time, we've got more company," Jake said.

"Well, this is gonna be fun," Dana said sarcastically.

They were going to just buy clothes and try and keep the location of Josephine's apartment a secret, but they assumed it would come out eventually. So they went back to the apartment and changed out of their wetsuits. Since Robben Island wasn't just a place you could simply access for free, Josephine bought online tickets for a tour on Robben Island, which in turn gave them access to the ferry they needed. It was getting late, so they needed to get there quickly.

While they were on the road again, squashed on the back seats and passing the aesthetically pleasing afternoon life of Cape Town, Ryan asked, "What is it exactly that you're expecting to do, Walker? Find the next treasure and then kill us when we're of no use to you?"

"That's exactly what's going to happen," Walker said.

"I think you'll find some difficulties in that task," Ryan said.

Walker turned around and looked Ryan dead in the eye and said, "We'll see about that."

Bradley hadn't said much since they were discovered at the beach. It was like the dynamics of his personality had changed ever since he was retaliated against in New Zealand. He didn't put up his somewhat respectable front, he just seemed plain evil. And Walker had a new wave of confidence, as if everything was in his control. Both of them were completely different, as if they had revealed their true selves.

"I've got a question for you, Walker," Jake said.

"Oh, do you now?" Walker said.

"Yes. What happened to all your men that clearly don't know what they're doing?" Jake asked.

"I sent them to finally remove the original concrete slab back in Sydney Harbour so no more idiots like yourself can follow us," Walker said, which was actually good news to Jake since he didn't want any other parties involved either.

"Alright, this is it," Josephine said, indicating that they had arrived at the ferry terminal.

There was barely any waiting line for the ferry and Dana questioned the reason for that.

"Robben Island isn't exactly a very beautiful place to go," Josephine said. "Sure, it's had rich history because of its famous maximum-security prison that's not running anymore, but overall, it's a very bland place that doesn't offer much value except for the view that looks back at Cape Town. Joseph Harrison certainly didn't choose it as a location for its desirability factors."

"Maybe what I said earlier was right. The lighthouse could provide a unique viewpoint that gives away the next location," Dana said.

"Let's hope you're right," Josephine said.

As they got there, they saw that Josephine was spot on. The island was very bland and the only nice part about it, and the ferry ride as well, was the view. But they weren't too concerned about the beauty factor. They just wanted to get to the lighthouse.

Once they got to the top, the view back to the city impressed them more than expected, especially with the incredible backdrop of Table Mountain and the overlaying rays of the setting sun.

"Ok, we need to look for the 'famous sound of the city,'" Jake said.

They scanned the city for a couple minutes because most of the buildings weren't exactly distinctive from the distance they were standing. After a little while longer, Josephine had a sudden realisation.

"You see that building that's somewhat isolated relative to the other buildings, with the roof that sticks out and comes to a point on the top?" Josephine asked.

"Yes, it absolutely sticks out," Jake said. "What about it?"

"That's City Hall, and inside the City Hall clock tower, is a massive bell that when rung, can be heard across much of Cape Town. It was built in 1905 and has become a famous landmark of Cape Town ever since," Josephine said. "I'm sure that's where we need to be."

"I think you're absolutely right," Jake said, much to the agreement of Dana and Ryan.

"Well then," Dana said. "Let's go to City Hall."

42. Calling In A Favour

"Getting into City Hall is not so simple," Josephine said as they were on the return ferry back towards the night lights of Cape Town.

"Why is that?" Jake asked.

"Because you can't just walk in. City Hall is very secure, and even if it doesn't look like its guarded, it always is," Josephine said.

"Then how do you get in?" Dana asked.

"The only way you can get in is if you're invited to one of the big events that is hosted at City Hall," Josephine said.

"Well, we're getting in there one way or another. I don't care how," Bradley said.

"Hold your horses, psychopath," Dana said.

Bradley was about to make a move on Dana, but Walker gestured for him to stay back, indicating that he wanted the discussion to continue.

"Anyway," Jake said, still keeping an eye on Bradley. "Is there a calendar that shows when all the events are on?"

"Yes, there is," Josephine said. "Give me a minute to look it up and I'll tell you when the next one is."

After a few clicks on her smartphone and some eye scanning on the information that seamlessly popped up, she found what she needed.

"Ok, I found it. The next event is the Cape Town Fashion Show, which fortunately, happens to be in two days," Josephine said.

"That sounds like a big event. Do you think we can get in?" Ryan asked.

"I happen to know someone that's taking part in the show. I'm sure I can convince her to take us as her guests," Josephine said.

"Just like that? So simple?" Dana asked.

"Let's just say that we used to be very close, and she owes me a favour from a while back," Josephine said mysteriously. "We won't have a problem getting in."

"That settles it then. Now all we have to do is wait and come up with a plan," Jake said.

43. Blueprints

The next night, they were all huddling around Josephine's dining room table, observing a set of blueprints for City Hall.

"Wait, how did you even get these?" Jake asked.

"I have a good friend who works in the county clerk's office who had no problem giving them to me," Josephine said.

"Does your network of contacts just expand over the entirety of Cape Town?" Dana asked.

Josephine shrugged. "More or less," she said. "That aside, we need to come up with a plan. Any suggestions?"

"Well, I assume the next treasure is up near the bell, at least according to the contents of the riddle," Ryan said.

"That assumption may or may not be correct," Jake said. "Harrison could've simply been pointing us to the building, not necessarily the bell."

"It's got to be pointing us towards the bell," Walker added. "It would be ridiculous to run around the entirety of City Hall trying to find a hidden treasure."

"Look at how many caves we had to explore before we found the *Ring of Valour*. I don't find it ridiculous at all," Dana said.

"Fine, that means we're stuck. What do you suppose, blondie?" Bradley said irritably much to Dana's displeasure.

"Ok relax," Jake said suddenly. "To be fair, I think Ryan and Walker are right."

"Why is that?" Dana asked.

"City Hall was built in 1905, well before Harrison finished the *Heists of Opulence*. By the time Harrison would've come to Cape Town to stash the next treasure, City Hall would've been very popular and guarded like it is today. Although he had to find an adequate hiding place, he wouldn't have had time to do anything too drastic or time consuming since he would've been discovered," Jake said. "So I would say that it's fair to narrow our location down to the vicinity of the bell."

"I see the logic in that," Dana said. "How do we get there? It's literally the highest point of the building."

"I've got an idea," Josephine said. "You see this large area here?" she asked, pointing to a large rectangular floor on the blueprints.

"Yeah, it looks like the central point of the hall, where people come together to chat and drink," Ryan said.

"That's exactly right. There are a couple staircases on each side since there are obviously multiple floors within the building. Those two stairwells simply lead to an upper floor which wouldn't get us to where we need to be. However, there is another staircase at the back, which leads to a restricted area. That staircase will be guarded, but if we can get past, we'll certainly get to where we need to be," Josephine explained.

"Basically, all we need is some kind of distraction to draw the guards away," Dana said.

"Exactly," Josephine said in agreement.

"Sounds easy enough," Ryan said. "I've already got multiple ideas."

"Ok, big man, tell us what we're gonna do," Jake said.

44. Preparations

Not even twenty-four hours later, they were all formally dressed and ready to attend the Cape Town Fashion Show in City Hall. Jake, Ryan, Walker and Bradley were all in traditional tuxes while Josephine and Dana were in short dresses for ease of mobility. The only differences between the two dresses were the colours. Josephine's dress was a deep green, the kind of colour only she could pull off. Dana opted for black, which Jake thought looked stunning on her.

As for the plan, Ryan would create some kind of distraction close to the staircase they needed to be. Ryan claimed that he would try to fake an argument with someone, or at least do something to attract attention to himself, drawing the guards away from the staircase. He wasn't too worried about the details since he would use his training instincts. Once the guard was drawn away, Jake and Walker agreed to go look for the next treasure together because they couldn't trust one another to go alone. The others would simply keep lookout, making sure nothing else went wrong.

"I guess it's not a terrible plan," Jake said.

"I think it's the best we've got since we don't know the internal environment of City Hall. We will have to work on the spot anyway," Dana said.

"Exactly," Ryan said.

Since they were all in agreement, they made their way down to the garage where Bradley's SUV and Josephine's Raptor was parked. They could've taken the Mitsubishi Lancer rental, but they only needed two cars anyway.

But before they got to the cars completely, Jake dropped back, and motioned Dana, Ryan and Josephine over to him.

"What is it?" Dana asked.

"Look," Jake said quietly. "We know that once we have the next treasure, Walker is going to try and kill us. So once he and I get past the guards and up the staircase, you three get out."

"We're not leaving you behind, it's absolutely out of the question. We're not arguing about this," Dana said.

Jake sighed at Dana's stubbornness, but then smiled, because that was one of the many things he loved about her.

"Ok, then what do you suggest?" Jake asked. "Because we have to get away from them as quickly as possible."

"What about choosing a meeting point?" Ryan said.

"That's more reasonable," Dana said. "Where are you thinking?"

"I was driving around and investigating the area yesterday, and I saw that there is a café just a block away from City Hall. It's open late and has a very distinctive neon sign outside. I say we try separate from Walker and Bradley and try to meet there," Ryan said. "Can you handle that?"

"For us that won't be much of a problem, but what about you, Jake? You've got to get the treasure *and* escape from Walker. How are you going to do that?" Dana asked.

"Leave that to me," Jake said confidently.

Bradley suddenly yelled from the SUV, "What's taking you so long?"

"Nothing. We're done," Jake said as they resumed their walk to Josephine's Raptor. "And Josephine, can I drive?"

"Sure. But if you so much as scratch this car, I'll kill you," Josephine said, only half-jokingly.

45. Runway Distractions

Jake drove Dana, Ryan and Josephine to City Hall for the fashion show, while Walker and Bradley followed suit in their SUV. There were cars and people everywhere, dressed to impress as expected, and there were excessive colourful lighting decorations all over the front of City Hall. It was so busy that it took them at least ten minutes to find available parking, and an additional while to locate Josephine's friend.

Josephine's friend was a tall, slim brunette who was wearing a long and flamboyant red dress, but she said that she would be changing multiple times for the runway show.

The runway show was the first and main event of the evening, so they were all directed to a section of the building that was separated from the central room of the hall, which had a few tables and drinks for now but remained relatively bare because of the attractions of the runway show. What really impressed them though, was the architecture, each structure so intricate and pleasing to the eye.

The runway show was starting soon, so Josephine's friend had to separate from them in order to dress and prepare for her multiple walks down the runway stage.

Jake was pleasantly surprised by the runway show. He admired the several outfits on display and enjoyed the music that the DJ was playing. Josephine's friend looked beautiful in all of her sequences of the show.

But Jake wasn't going to let the show distract him from the fact that they had a job to do, so he turned to Dana and said, "Come with me, I've got an idea."

Dana obliged and Jake took her hand, slipping away from Walker and Bradley, leading her out of the crowded runway hall and back into the central room. To their left, on the far side of the room was the staircase they needed, and they were right, it was guarded, but there was only one guard on that staircase.

"Ok, let's go up to him and ask him where the bathroom is," Jake said quietly. "You pretend that you really need to use it."

"Why should I be the one pretending?" Dana asked cheekily, with her hands on her hips.

"Because of your feminine charm," Jake said jokingly.

"Oh really?"

"Just do it," Jake said. "Besides, I'm the one going up anyway, and if I could get up there now without Walker, that would be great."

"Alright, Jakey, let's do this."

They walked up to the guard and Dana said, "Hi there, I'm looking for the bathroom. This is my boyfriend; he's just accompanying me because it would be rude to let his dear girlfriend walk alone in a strange place. Anyway, can you please tell me where it is? I really need to go," Dana said in the sweetest tone ever.

Jake found it hard not to laugh at the script Dana just came up with for herself, but he managed to stay calm.

"Right this way, ma'am," the guard said in a heavy South African accent.

As the guard was leading Dana in the other direction, Jake tried to subtly double back, sensing an easy opportunity, but the guard turned around and saw Jake doing this.

"Hey! What are you doing?" the guard said.

"Just admiring the architecture," Jake said casually.

"Yeah, right," the guard said sarcastically. "Get over here, and there's the bathroom," he said, pointing to the left near the entrance hall, and then giving Jake a little shove in that direction.

"Well, we tried. Thanks," Jake said to Dana when the guard was out of earshot. "I particularly liked the girlfriend act," he said playfully.

"Yeah it was fun," Dana said. "It was a shame we couldn't get you in though," she said truthfully.
"It's alright. Let's regroup with the others and come up with something."

"Wait, I think I might just have the perfect idea."

46. A Drunken Act

Before Jake could ask what her idea was, there was an announcement stating that the main attraction was shifting to the central room of the hall, where Jake and Dana just came from. The announcement included that there were to be food and drinks served on the side, while the DJ would be playing soft music. The crowd dispersed and soon the central room was transformed in a matter of a couple minutes, with couples dancing in the centre, and waiters serving at the side.

"It's going to be a lot harder getting access to the staircase with all this exposure," Jake said to the group.

"This doesn't totally change the plan I came up with a couple minutes ago," Dana said. "It just slows it down slightly."

"Ok, walk us through it," Josephine said.

"With the addition of the crowd, Jake and I can dance to try and blend in because the guard is already somewhat suspicious of us" Dana said. "Then Josephine, you simply go up to the guard and talk to him. Then Dad, you stumble toward the man, acting drunk and start a fight with him. It might get you kicked out, but it will buy Jake and Walker enough time to get past. It has to be you, Dad, because if Bradley gets kicked out, he has no idea what we're up to. When I nod to you, make your move."

"That's a pretty clever plan," Josephine said.

"Whatever, just do it. We're losing time," Bradley said impatiently.

Jake and Dana made their way to the centre of the room, joining the slow dancing couples. Jake outstretched his left arm and held Dana's hand in his, while Jake's other hand rested on her waist; a typical waltzing structure. They danced together smoothly as one.

"Back in the Botanical Gardens, did you expect to be doing this in the midst of a treasure hunt?" Jake asked.

"No I didn't," Dana said. "But it's a pleasantly surprising addition."

Jake smiled. He overheard an old English couple next to them use an expression he hadn't heard in a long time.

"That's preposterous, darling," Jake said softly and cheerfully to Dana, mocking the English couple.

Dana laughed. "That expression is going to become permanent with you from now on, isn't it?"

"Very much so," Jake said.

They continued dancing for another two minutes when finally, they saw Josephine strike a conversation with the guard. After about fifteen seconds of conversation, Dana nodded to Ryan, indicating that he should put on his act.

Ryan pretendedly stumbled over to Josephine and the guard and yelled, "Hey! Who do you think you're talking to? Get away from her!"

The guard raised his arms slightly and said, "Sir, calm down."

Ryan stumbled closer. "I said, get away from her!" And he threw a wild but sloppy punch.

Josephine got out of the way quickly and the guard ducked, then shoved Ryan away from him. He then started dragging Ryan towards the City Hall entrance, the opposite end of the staircase. Ryan obviously could've fought the guard in his sleep, but this was all part of the objective.

Jake separated from Dana and linked up with Walker, both of them discretely making their way closer to the staircase, and they successfully got there undetected.

47. Maze Navigation

Jake and Walker bolted up the stairs to the next floor only to find that they had three choices. They could go left or right down expansive corridors, or they could go up another flight of stairs. They didn't know if there were any more guards stationed around the building, so once again, they had to move fast. Yet each path was unfamiliar to them.

"Which way?" Walker asked.

"We need to keep going go up, so let's try the stairs," Jake said decisively.

"What if this doesn't lead to the bell?" Walker asked.

"Then we find a way that does. Now let's go!" Jake yelled hurriedly.

They rushed up the stairs only to find that there was another corridor split, but not another staircase going up to another floor. But the floor they reached did give way to an open view of City Hall, which allowed them to orientate themselves.

"Ok, we're still on the outskirts of the building," Jake said analytically. "There's the clock tower in the centre, and we know for a fact that the bell is in there, hanging at the top. Both paths here look identical, let's go right!"

They sprinted down the corridor, suits of metal armour and ancient paintings flashing by as they ran past. When they reached the end of the corridor, they had to make a left, which took them closer to the clock tower.

As they ran further, they heard a couple voices up ahead, and Jake knew it was only a matter of seconds before he saw guards turn the corner in front of them and spot them, so he instinctively dived into the open room to his right, and Walker quickly followed.

They realised they were in some sort of reading space, with an expensive looking desk and furniture and numerous book shelves.

They hid behind some furniture pieces and waited for the guards to pass. When Jake thought the coast was clear, he edged toward the doorway, but then he shortly heard the same voices again, so he pressed himself against the wall.

As they passed by again, Jake silently cursed. "I think they're patrolling this area," he said to Walker when the guards were out of earshot. "We need to find another way, perhaps through that door behind you."

"What if there are people in there?" Walker asked.

Jake edged toward the door and placed his head against it, in an attempt to eavesdrop. "I don't hear anyone. Besides, everyone should be downstairs in the main event anyway."

"Ok, open it quietly," Walker said.

Jake did as he was told and as expected, there weren't any people in the room. So they carried on, creeping through, room by room.

As they passed through the last room which seemed to be some kind of office with high-tech equipment, they noticed that there was no interleading door to another room, just the door that led back to the corridor. They heard that the guards were just outside so they waited a few seconds before they walked far enough away to the left.

Jake opened the door and raced to the right, finally seeing the entrance to the clock tower which was just another left turn away. Jake turned the corner so quickly that he nearly knocked over another suit of armour, but luckily got away unscathed.

"Watch where you're going next time," Walker said. But they weren't too concerned, because they had reached the clock tower, and all they had to do was climb another set of stairs and a ladder, and they would reach the bell.

48. Rust

The set of stairs led Jake and Walker to a large room in the shape of a perfect square, with huge windows nearly spanning the height of the room, providing a three-sixty-degree view around City Hall. Depending on where they looked, they could see everything; the ocean, Table Mountain, the entrance of the building where the main event was being held, and the expanse of city lights across Cape Town.

But they didn't come to admire the view, so they climbed the ladder which was just short of ten meters high. When they reached the top, they stepped onto a platform that was part of a cramped room that housed the workings of the clock, and the massive bell was dangling in the centre, attached to wrap around metal which connected to a wooden support beam near the roof.

"Um, this does not look like a place where you could hide treasure," Walker said.

"Patience, Walker, patience," Jake said. "Joseph Harrison wouldn't have just left it lying around for someone to take. Look for anything that seems unnatural for this room, like an indentation on the wall. It's all in the details. The truth is always there, you just need to look for it."

"Yeah, spare me the essay. Let's just look," Walker said.

They didn't have much space to work with, and they had to be careful to not touch the complicated workings of the clock. Jake scanned every ounce of the room to try and notice any small detail that popped out to him. After a few minutes, the task was starting to seem impossible to him, because most of the room was either wood or brick and no section looked particularly different from another.

But then, just as hope was starting to fade, he saw something strange.

"Walker," Jake said. "Do you see where the bell is held at the top?"

"What about it?" Walker asked.

"Just above the bell itself, there's something that's sticking out of the wooden support beam. It looks like a handle of some sort, and it doesn't have any function for the room" Jake said.

"We can't exactly pull it," Walker said. "We would need to come back with tools to unhook the bell and we don't have time for that."

"Well, it's the only thing that looks out of place to me," Jake said. "We have to try, or I will at least."

Jake managed to grip himself on one of the edge walls and climbed a couple meters, which was all he needed, and then, missing the workings of the clock,

Jake daringly jumped across from the wall and grabbed onto the top wooden support beam. It was then he noticed that parts of the wraparound metal had rusted, specifically the sections that bent over the wood, the most vital connection point.

"That's just a bit alarming," Jake said.

But without further hesitation, with one hand, he grabbed onto the handle-like object that stuck out between the bottom of the wood and the top of the bell, and he pulled it. Mostly, it seemed stuck, but he swore he saw about a millimetre of movement.

So he yanked it with all his might, and everything happened at once. He pulled it out so hard that he ended up smashing his arm on the bell with such force that caused the rusted wraparound metal to snap, causing the bell to fall toward the floor below, and Jake with it. As Jake was falling, he managed to snatch one of the ladder rungs with his free hand, just before the bell hit the floor with the most deafening of rings. He closed his eyes at the painful piercing of the sound and because of the pain he was experiencing in his left arm. When he opened his eyes again, he realised that in his left hand, he was still holding the object he intended to get.

He was holding a sword that was still dangerously sharp and the edge of the silver blade was encrusted with diamonds and red zircons, just like the *Ring of Valour*. It was the most beautiful and striking sword he had ever seen, and he knew it was the famous sword known as the *Sword of Capacity,* stolen during the *Heists of Opulence.* He was shocked by the fact that he found it and was holding it, and he was amazed that he didn't slice his arm open on the way down.

But he suddenly heard the fast approach of voices and footsteps.

49. The Last Clue

With the sword, Jake leapt to the floor and ran as fast as he could down the stairs, wanting to get away from both the guards, and Walker. When he reached the corridor at the bottom of the stairs, he looked to his left and saw multiple guards running towards him.

He looked back and saw Walker storming down the stairs after him who shouted, "Don't even think about it, Jake!"

Jake knew the deadly consequences if he stayed with Walker, so Jake dashed to his right in the only direction that he could. He had no idea how to get back to the entrance, so his only priority for now was to run and not get caught. The sword was heavy, and his arm was already aching, but the adrenalin helped him keep up his speed. As he was nearing the end of the corridor, he saw that the corridor ended and he needed to make another left, but more guards had just arrived, blocking off his only path. He was about to panic, but he noticed that there was a large window at the end of the corridor. All he could see outside the window was the black night sky and a protruding section of the building about sixty meters away. But it being his only option, he sprinted at the window as hard as he could.

And he jumped.

As he hit the window, the glass shattered, and shards of glass flew everywhere. He looked down and saw that there was a large drop to a balcony deck below. He landed hard on his side and forced himself into a sideways roll, so he didn't get hit by the sword.

Jake looked behind him and saw that the guards hadn't made the jump and were shouting at him, but they quickly moved out of the way and suddenly, someone emerged. It was Walker, flying through the now windowless gap down to the balcony deck Jake was standing on.

Jake quickly looked around to analyse his options. He couldn't climb up to the roof and the drop down to the ground was too high. But he saw a very expansive flag hanging down the length of the building just below the balcony deck.

So, Jake instinctively hopped over the balcony railing and then flung himself toward the flag below. He bear hugged the flag with all the strength he had, careful not to stab himself with the sword.

He was sliding down the flag at a rapid rate and his arms were burning like hell. When Jake couldn't bare the pain any longer, he dropped to the floor and landed heavily on his back.

Fortunately, the drop wasn't that high, but he was still exhausted and breathless. When he looked up, he saw no sign of Walker. Jake rolled over and again, heard the sound of running footsteps, so he forced himself up, grabbed the sword, and bolted towards the street in the other direction.

As he got to the street, he looked to his right and saw that someone was speeding towards him in an immensely loud Aston Martin Rapid AMR, but suddenly stopped right in front of him.

Dana was in the driver seat and Ryan was next to her in the passenger seat.

"Get in!" Dana shouted.

Jake rushed into the back seat and as he closed the door, Dana sped off.

"Where on Earth is Josephine?" Jake asked in exhaustion.

"No idea. We told her we were leaving, and she totally vanished. So we came to rescue you," Dana said with her foot to the floor.

"Thank you. But how did you get this car? And I thought we had a meeting point," Jake said.

"Yeah, that changed when you caused all that chaos," Ryan said. "We had to make another plan quickly, so I saw this rich douchebag and claimed I was an officer and needed his car. Too bad he didn't know I don't have any jurisdiction here. And Dana insisted on driving," he said as he saw the sword. "Beautiful sword. Is that writing engraved on the blade?"

Jake looked at the blade and Ryan was right. Jake didn't notice it before because it was so subtle.

"What does it say?" Ryan asked.

What my grave faces and what my sigil presents.

Jake understood the riddle instantly and was about to explain it to Dana and Ryan. But as they entered an intersection, Dana barely had time to react to what was coming, and another car crashed into them from an adjacent road. The Aston Martin spun several times before hitting a wall head on.

50. Out Of Options

The front end of the Aston Martin was crumpled and the engine was smoking. Jake, Dana and Ryan were dazed from the blow to the wall, and it took them a few moments to recover.

"I thought the intersection was clear. That's why I kept going," Dana said.

"That crash wasn't your fault," Jake said. "But it wasn't an accident either."

"What do you mean by that?" Ryan asked.

But that question didn't need answering, because as they all looked to their right, they saw someone stepping out of a Dodge RAM with bull bars attached to the front bumper; clearly the car that hit them. Out of the driver seat stepped a familiar looking athletic woman with striking black hair, an unblemished facial structure and intense green eyes.

It was Josephine.

And soon after, Bradley stepped out of the passenger seat, and Walker out of the back.

"No," Jake said, unable to accept what was happening, finding it hard to breath or move.

Josephine and Bradley were walking towards them with pistols in their hands.

"Get out of the car," Josephine said.

Dana and Ryan slowly obliged but Jake couldn't. He was still too shocked.

"Did you not hear her?" Bradley shouted. "She said, get out of the car!" And he opened the door and yanked Jake out onto the floor.

For a brief moment, Jake had wondered how they had got to them so fast, but then he remembered that Josephine lived in Cape Town and knew the streets better than anyone.

Jake finally got to his feet and looked Josephine dead in the eye. "Why?" he asked, his voice trembling.

"It's not personal," Josephine said casually. "Walker offered me a lot of money for this."

"What about everything you've done for us?" Dana asked. "Like saving us from those thieves, taking us to the HMS Invictus and Robben Island, and helping us get to this point."

"Saving you was genuine, because I hate some of the scum that roam this place. But everything else was all just to build your trust. I've been connected to Walker for years, and as soon as I found out who you were, it was a lucky coincidence, and I acted on it," Josephine said.

Jake now understood why Walker knew about their whereabouts in Cape Town, and why he was so confident and at ease with life since they met at the

Cape of Good Hope. It was because Walker had a constant feed of inside information.

"So, you don't care about being a part of history? It's only about money to you," Jake said with raw emotion in his voice.

"It's about the money for everyone. Sooner or later you'll realise that," Josephine said, much to Jake's disappointment.

"Alright, that's enough chatter, hand us the sword," Bradley said, while Walker was still calmly leaning against the truck.

Jake's instinct was to wildly swing the sword at Bradley in defiance, and he was about to do just that. But then he remembered what happened the last time he retaliated in a situation like this; he almost got Dana and Ryan killed.

So in defeat, and out of options, Jake handed the sword over to Bradley.

"Good choice," Bradley said.

"Now," Walker said. "Finish the job I'm paying you for, Josephine."

"No problem," Josephine said, and she stepped forward and knocked Dana and Ryan to the floor, restrained them, and threw them in the back of the Dodge.

"What are you doing?" Jake asked.

"Remember how I said I was going to kill you at this point?" Walker asked. "Well, I figured there was something better to do. I'm taking what you love, and you can't do anything about it."

Josephine then walked to Jake and punched him hard in the stomach, causing him to double over.

Walker went to retrieve a silver briefcase from the boot of the car and handed it to Josephine.

"Pleasure doing business with you, Josephine," Walker said.

"And you, Walker. If you ever need anything again, give me a call," Josephine said.

"Will do," Walker said as he got into the car. He looked at Jake and said, "See you never," and he drove off.

Josephine then stepped forward and said, "Night, night," before delivering a kick to Jake's face, knocking him unconscious, and Josephine walked off into the night.

51. Raptor

Jake woke up next to a pile of blood on the floor, which he assumed was from a nasty nosebleed he had while he was unconscious, because it felt like his nose was broken.

Aside from seeing a few low-key residential buildings around him and some street lights posted on the sidewalk, he had lost his bearings which was alarming due to the dangerous, crime-filled night life of Cape Town.

To make matters worse, he had learnt his lesson from when they got stopped by the thieves on their first night in Cape Town, so he tried not to do anything drastic and dangerous this time for the sake of Dana and Ryan's safety. But somehow, Jake had still gotten himself into this ever daunting and helpless situation with no idea what to do next.

He tried to theorise where Walker and Bradley would be heading to next, and then he remembered the engraving on the *Sword of Capacity*.

What my grave faces and what my sigil presents.

When Jake had originally read that in the back of the Aston Martin Rapid AMR, he didn't have time to explain to Dana and Ryan that Joseph Harrison was leading them to the Sydney Harbour Bridge.

Jake knew this because Harrison's grave had a prime view of Sydney Harbour, directly facing the Sydney Harbour Bridge. And Jake knew that Harrison's sigil had the design of an anchor and diagonal lines behind it. Jake instantly envisioned the lines representing the bottom of the Sydney Harbour Bridge, as if one were looking at it from the perspective of the water beneath it.

And that's how he knew that he needed to get there, in the city where this whole journey began, and that's where Walker and Bradley would be heading right now, if they had figured it out, which Jake assumed they had.

I need to get to the airport, Jake thought.

But he also thought that the local police would've placed an alert on Walker and Bradley, and *himself* as well. So he knew that they would have difficulties getting through the airport, unless they somehow used personal aircraft services. Anything was possible with Walker's money and connections.

Nonetheless, Jake's decision about the airport had not changed. The only problem was that he had no idea how to get there, and he couldn't get there quick enough without an available car.

The longer he thought about his situation, the more helpless he felt.

And then he remembered another situation, a long time ago, where he felt hopeless and thought his and Dana's mixed basketball team was going to lose the championship *because of him*, and Dana said to him, "If you don't believe in yourself, who else will?'"

Her words cleared Jake's mind, and suddenly, he felt that he still had Josephine's car keys in his pocket. He knew that Josephine would be back to retrieve what was rightfully hers. So, while Jake was backtracking his path back to City Hall in search for the Raptor, he had to be weary of his surroundings in case Josephine showed up, or in case any dangers of the night life presented themselves.

But nothing would stop his determination.

Dana, Ryan, I'm coming for you, he thought.

52.   Airfield

Jake managed to get to the Ford Raptor unscathed and was surprised to see that many people were still partying at City Hall.

He felt worlds away from that party.

He got in the car and used the convenient GPS instalment to guide him to the airport. There was no use trying to sneak back to Josephine's apartment, because he knew Walker would've picked up all of the belongings, including the *Ring of Valour*. So, Jake sped the whole way to the airport because of the desperate circumstances and because he couldn't afford to get stopped or mugged by anyone. At one point, Jake was going so fast that as he turned a tight corner, he lost grip on the rear end, causing the car to slide. But his immense focus allowed him to easily stabilise the car and he continued advancing towards the airport.

When Jake got there, he found a dirt road that snaked around the outside fence of the airport. He used it to start a search for a private runway.

It took Jake a while to find what he was looking for due to the sheer size of the airport, but sure enough, he found an isolated aircraft hangar. In that hangar was a familiar Dodge RAM that was parked next to a cargo plane. Jake saw that Walker, Bradley and a few other men were loading cargo crates onto the back of the plane.

Jake was confused as to why they needed a cargo plane, but with Walker's extensive operational network, he thought that Walker could've very well come to Cape Town to do more than one job with extra manpower at his disposal.

But Jake brushed that thought away because he saw Dana and Ryan on the floor, restrained and helpless. When the cargo crates were packed, Bradley walked over to Ryan and Dana, dragged them to the back of the plane and shoved them inside with the cargo crates. Once everyone was inside, the motors of the plane had fired up and the plane started moving. Jake knew he had to do something fast, or else the chances of saving Dana and Ryan would vanish.

Jake suddenly had a crazy idea and he thought that as far as ideas go, this was the most dangerous one so far. He backed up the Raptor and when he thought his distance from the fence was long enough, he stopped, used the gear lever to ensure the car would drive forwards and not backwards, and planted his foot on the accelerator as hard as he could, ramming the fence.

The linkage of the fence he crashed into went flying into the air and bounced off the roof of the car. He didn't care if it raised an alarm within the airport since he solely focused on catching up with the plane.

He didn't have much time before the plane gained more speed than he did, so kept his foot to the floor, the night lights of the airport flashing by faster and faster. He was driving so fast that one wrong move would unsettle the car into a violent spin. Jake kept his cool and gained on the cargo plane quickly.

He drove underneath the plane and pulled to the left of the front wheel, opened his door, stood up, and still kept his foot on the accelerator. Sensing the plane was speeding up, he instinctively leaped out of the car and onto the segment that connected the wheel to the plane. It was a miracle that he even made the jump, because if he touched the wheel, he would've been done for.

The plane was going incredibly fast now, and he was holding on as tight as he could for dear life, and suddenly, the plane was in the air.

The ground was dropping away from him and he could quickly see rooftops of buildings and the night lights of Cape Town, everything in view getting further and further away. He could feel the wheel retracting into the body of the plane. His whole body was aching from the sheer force he was using to keep himself from falling, but just as the wheel completely retracted and the plane had closed up, he was able to let go.

As he let go he didn't even fall since he noticed that he was in very tight space that seemed to connect to other parts of the plane with a ventage system. Jake didn't exactly know how to navigate his way to Dana and Ryan, but he felt triumphant to even make it to this point.

    Now it was up to him to find them.

53. Eavesdropping

The closest vent opening to Jake was directly behind him. It would be a tight crawl, but he didn't have much of a choice. He set on his crawl through the dark vent to spot any sort of light or opening which would help him figure out where he was in relation to Dana and Ryan.

He followed the vent for what felt like ages in such a cramped space, and at once stage he ended up whacking his head on the top of the vent due to a wave of turbulence. But after crawling for several minutes, he finally spotted some light up ahead, so he moved towards it.

The light was above him and he came to realise that he was under the flooring of the main cargo deck. His view was slightly obscured by a cargo crate with some sort of netting wrapped around it, but he could see a couple guards chatting to each other. He focused his hearing on the guards.

"I tell you man, working for Walker is not easy," the one guard said. "He may pay us well, but he thinks that his authority gives him the right to be disrespectful."

"Yeah, not to mention that Bradley often goes to extremes as well," the other guard said. "But what have Walker and Bradley been doing on the side anyway? What has driven them to kidnap these two people and bring them with us?" he said, pointing towards the front of the cargo deck, which Jake assumed was possibly where Dana and Ryan were held.

"I don't know, but it seems like Walker's line of work creates a lot of enemies. If he's not careful, he's gonna get hit where it hurts. I just hope us two are not around when that happens."

Tough luck, buddy, Jake thought.

He tried to get his head as close to the flooring as possible to try and see if Dana and Ryan were there, and sure enough, he could just make out Dana's blonde hair behind one of the crates. Now that he knew the location of Dana and Ryan, all he had to do was bide his time before all hell broke loose.

Waiting several hours in a cramped vent, what could possibly be more fun than this? Jake thought sarcastically.

54. Crate Chaos

Many hours later, Jake could see small streaks of daylight coming through the plane windows, but Jake was dehydrated, his body had many cramps because his freedom of movement was severely limited in the ventage system, and he was very uncomfortable from the lack of opportunities to go to the bathroom.

But his adrenalin had quickly kicked in because he heard the voices of Walker and Bradley from the cargo deck above, announcing they were to begin their descent.

Suddenly, the crate above Jake shifted from the plane's movements, which would allow him to easily pop open the floor panel that he was lying beneath.

"Go sort that out," Walker said, as he and Bradley retreated back into the main quarters of the plane.

The guard started walking in Jake's direction. As the guard got closer, Jake crept back into the shadows so the guard wouldn't see him.

Here we go, Jake thought.

As the guard grabbed onto the crate, Jake sprung up from underneath the floor panel and aimed a rapid uppercut at the guard's skull. The guard instantly fell to the floor and Jake grabbed the pistol from the guard's waist strap, and aimed it at the second guard, all in the matter of a couple seconds.

The second guard was completely bewildered at what just happened, and so were Dana and Ryan, who Jake could now see clearly, restrained to seating against the frame of the plane.

"Now," Jake said to the guard. "I want you to cut them loose, slowly."

While the guard did what he was told, Jake took a look out the window to see where they were. They were currently flying over Sydney city.

After the guard cut Dana and Ryan loose, they moved to Jake's side and he said, "Now hand me that backpack on the wall," assuming it was the backpack with the treasure inside.

Jake inspected the contents of the backpack and he was right; the *Ring of Valour* and *Sword of Capacity* were both there.

Jake thought the only reason why Walker didn't leave the bag in a more secure place was to dangle it in front of Dana and Ryan for psychological torture. But while Jake was distracted, the guard quickly pressed a big red button, sounding an emergency alarm across the plane.

Multiple guards came rushing to the scene to investigate the problem, then came Walker and Bradley. Jake, Dana and Ryan were now completely surrounded and were forced against the frame of the plane.

"Ok," Walker said, eyeing Jake. "It's simply impossible for you to be here right now."

"You only think that because you underestimated him," Dana said aggressively.

Walker walked towards them and menacingly said, "You think you're so much better than me? Well, look where you are. This lame attempt of a rescue has gotten you fools nowhere."

"You shouldn't be so sure about that," Ryan said confidently.

Suddenly Bradley intervened. "And why's that? You think you've got some kind of trick up your sleeve? I know you too well. You've got nothing."

"Like I said, you shouldn't be so sure about that," Ryan repeated, and he leant against the frame of the plane, pulling a release lever.

The door of the plane dropped open and many of the guards scattered out of the way for the fear of falling out.

"Enough with the theatrics," Walker said. "I should've just stuck to my original plan and killed all of you." And he pulled out his pistol.

But suddenly, Dana yanked on a handle attached to the cargo crate next to them, which deployed an open parachute. Jake and Ryan, quickly realising Dana's intentions, grabbed onto the wraparound netting of the crate with her, Jake being careful not to lose the backpack, and they were sucked out of the plane and into the air.

The crate quickly stabilised and settled into a calm descent, but then Jake used his pistol to shoot at the motors of the plane. After several shots, smoke started to billow from both wings of the plane, unsettling the flight path and causing it to dive.

But then someone jumped out of the plane and skydived towards the crate that Jake, Dana and Ryan were holding on to.

"Who on Earth is insane enough to do that?" Jake yelled.

"It's Walker!" Dana yelled in response.

And Walker's aim was spot on. He was approaching at speed, but he managed to grab onto the netting, unsettling the motion of the crate, causing it to drop quicker.

Walker climbed to the top of the crate and said, "I've had enough of you three! It's time to end this!"

"What are you gonna do, Walker?" I've got my pistol aimed at you," Jake said.

But Walker was too quick for Jake to react, and in no time at all, Walker used a concealed knife to cut the rope connecting the parachute to the crate.

Walker jumped off the crate and out of nowhere, someone else was skydiving too. It was Bradley. He caught Walker and deployed his own parachute, and

Walker gave Jake, Dana and Ryan an evil smile, before they started spiralling and plummeting down towards the ground, over the rooftops of the northern suburbs of Sydney.

55. A Rough Landing

They could see they were heading straight towards a hill that led down to a beach. They were all struggling to hold on because of the rapid downward motion and the intense force of air resistance.

"Listen!" Ryan shouted. "We are not gonna die! We're heading straight for that hill. Hold on for as long as you can and then let go and aim for the beach!"

Even in an incredible freefall, Jake and Dana looked over to each other and nodded, as if to say, "We've got this."

"Here we go!" Ryan shouted, as they were closing in.

And they smashed into the top of the hill. The front half of the crate broke apart immediately, sending weapons and explosives flying out of the crate in random directions. But the other half of the crate remained relatively intact, carrying the three of them into a terrifying slide at hair-raising speed.

The now half-crate suddenly hit a rock, causing it to flip in to a series of violent vertical spins. After several rotations, it flew across a walkway, banging in to the walkway railing, at which point, Jake, Dana and Ryan let go, and were ejected towards the beach.

They all landed hard on the sand and their extreme momentum carried them into a sequence of rolls, until finally, a significant distance later, they became stationary.

Jake lay still momentarily, dazed from the pain of several grazes and hits, and even from dizziness. Somehow his ears were ringing, he had sand in his eyes, his hair was windblown, and the tux he was still wearing was almost shredded. Luckily the *Ring of Valour* and *Sword of Capacity* were still intact.

Jake slowly got up to check on Dana and Ryan, who suffered similar outcomes. He looked up and saw a cloud of smoke in the distance, probably from the cargo plane that had crashed.

They stayed silent for a few minutes, catching their breath and regaining their composure, until Dana said, "Alright, we have to get moving. Walker could be at the Harbour Bridge by now."

"Ok," Jake said. "I have a plan, and you're not gonna like it."

56. A Daring Decision

Jake paid a fellow civilian to let him use her Mini Cooper. The lady was quite sceptical but agreed as long as she could stay in the car. So, he raced to the Harbour Bridge and the woman was very displeased with how Jake drove since he was driving incredibly fast and took each corner with intense precision, just within the bounds of the road.

When he got to his destination beneath the Harbour Bridge, he handed the keys over to the lady who hastily drove off, and Jake prepared to climb the bridge. He knew from the riddle that he needed to be on the underside of the bridge, and he assumed he needed to be at the centre because that was the most inaccessible spot. So, that's where he would climb, alone and without the support of Dana and Ryan.

Jake looked up and noticed he had to climb a bit of the viewing tower first, and then cross over onto the metal support segments of the bridge, from which he could crawl upwards.

It was very challenging climbing up the viewing tower since there were barely any footholds and he could only hang on by his fingertips with little support from his toes. He was soaked in sweat only two minutes into the climb.

People were starting to gather on the grass beneath, and Jake heard someone say, "Why does he not have any climbing gear like the other two?"

Jake immediately looked around the viewing tower and saw that Walker and Bradley had come from the other side and were already climbing up the metal segments on the actual bridge, using somewhat secure harnesses that they could attach where needed.

Jake now had a boost of adrenalin and continued climbing the viewing tower at impossible pace. He then hopped over onto the metal segments and began crawling upwards, and quickly.

Walker then spotted Jake and made eye contact with him, anger flushing across his face. "You should be dead from that crate impact! And to make matters worse, you destroyed my plane and all my cargo! But you know what? It doesn't matter, because once I get my hands on this treasure, and take back the ones you stole, I'll finally put a bullet in your skull. No one will know who you are, and I'll become a hero with infinite value!"

Jake kept crawling upwards and towards the centre of the bridge. "That's a nice fantasy you have," he said coolly.

"Alright, let's just get the treasure and then get rid of this pathetic imbecile," Bradley said.

"I agree," Walker said.

And the three of them raced toward the centre of the bridge. While Walker and Bradley had to regularly stop to disconnect and reconnect their harness points, Jake pulled ahead because he didn't need to do that.

Once Jake reached the top and could no longer crawl, he gripped onto the horizontal metal support beams and swung across each one, as if he was using monkey bars, high above the water and the passing boats of the harbour. One wrong move would have fatal consequences, but he wasn't going to let Walker win this time.

As Jake got to what he felt like was the centre of the bridge, he looked around for any unique indentation or marking left by Joseph Harrison. After a couple minutes, Jake came to see a slight carving of a circle, and within the circle was the familiar design of an anchor with diagonal lines behind it; Harrison's sigil.

Jake swung his legs up and hooked them around the bar in front of him for extra support. He then got a closer look and saw that this piece of metal, although attached to the bridge, was still a separate piece. And one part of the sigil, the anchor, didn't look like it was metal at all, it looked like silver. The silver extended into a small square marking within the sigil that jutted out slightly.

Instinctively, Jake pressed on the silver square and nothing happened. But then he pressed on it with more force and suddenly, the sigil broke, and what fell out of the sigil was a silver cross, with the anchor at its base. The cross was visually stunning, perhaps even more stunning than the *Ring of Valour* or the *Sword of Capacity*, also encrusted with diamonds and red zircons. Jake recognised the cross to be the *Cross of Faith*, the last piece of the trinity of treasures from Joseph Harrison's *Heists of Opulence*.

Jake was transfixed.

But then Walker was suddenly a couple meters to his right, and Bradley to Jake's left.

"Give it up, Jake," Walker said. "You've got nowhere to go and once again, you have no choice but to give it to us."

"That's where you're wrong," Jake said. "I learnt from my mistakes and came here alone. I didn't put Dana and Ryan in the danger of you, which means you don't have any leverage against me. You're the one that's out of options."

"You're wrong. We could just *push* you off," Bradley said.

"But then you'd have to search the harbour and that would take ages," Jake said.

"That's only a slight annoyance with the team I have at my disposal," Walker said. "In fact, I think we will push you off."

Jake gave out an evil smile and said, "As you wish."

And he let go, taking a long dive down into the water of the harbour.

57. Outwitted

Jake had emerged at McMahon's Point with Dana, observing Sydney Harbour, and waving and attracting the attention of Walker and Bradley, who were now climbing down the Harbour Bridge.

Dana looked at Jake and smiled. "That really was a dangerous plan, but it worked. And look, they're on their way here now."

"Right where we want them to be."

"Now we wait."

Only five minutes later, Walker and Bradley sped into the carpark at McMahon's point. They got out of their car and angrily marched towards Jake and Dana, but suddenly, they shook in place and fell to the ground.

It was Ryan who had appeared behind and used a taser gun on them.

"Aren't you forgetting something?" Ryan asked, as they lay on the ground, still shocked from the electricity. "We're back in Sydney, where I'm chief of police. These are my streets."

As he was handcuffing them, he said, "You're under arrest. Anything you say can and will be used against you in the court of law," and carried on explaining their rights before he threw them into the police vehicle.

Before they drove off, Walker said, "Wait. I at least want to know how you survived that fall in the harbour and got here so quickly."

"Well, it's quite simple. I stalled you two long enough before the Fast Manly Ferry came past, and that's when I jumped. The ferry generated enough waves and disturbance to break the concrete surface of the water. As I landed in the water, Dana was already waiting beneath the surface with a sea scooter, which we quickly directed here. Then, as you idiots rushed over, we had Ryan come up behind you, and you know the rest," Jake explained.

Walker looked dejected and embarrassed while Bradley looked severely angry.

"See you never, Walker," Dana said cheekily.

"Dana, Jake, chat later," Ryan said, giving a nod of farewell before driving off.

"Well," Dana said, smiling at Jake. "Now that we've completed the modern version of the *Heists of Opulence*, what happens now?"

"There's still a few things we need to do."

58. New Beginnings

Jake and Dana ended up reporting their findings to the Australian government. They received a generous payment for doing so and the *Ring of Valour*, *Sword of Capacity*, and *Cross of Faith* were all placed in a museum in the city of Sydney. Beneath the display of treasures, there was an inscription featuring their names and how they adventurously completed the modern *Heists of Opulence*, orchestrated by the most infamous pirate of all time; Joseph Harrison.

Jake and Dana became a part of history.

Once all was said and done, Jake and Dana took a stroll in the Botanical Gardens, to reflect on everything that happened, where it all started.

They came across peaceful piano music being played amongst the greenery, and Jake said, "Care for a dance?"

"Certainly, my dear Jakey," Dana said friendly.

Once again, Jake outstretched his left arm and held Dana's hand in his, while Jake's other hand rested on her waist; a typical waltzing structure.

They smoothly danced together for several minutes in reflective silence, until Jake asked, "You know what Walker's problem was?"

"What?"

"He was driven by profit, but treasure hunting isn't just about profit. It's about the moments you form while doing so."

Dana smiled and said, "I couldn't agree with you more."

Dana then leant her head against Jake's shoulder, and they danced together a little while longer, before Dana said, "What are we gonna do now? Finish school and get on with our careers? Because there's certainly no way I'm settling for an office job after this."

"Yeah, that sounds kind of preposterous, darling," Jake said in a fake English accent, in reminiscence of the similar moment they had in Cape Town. "But I'm sure we'll find something that satisfies us."

Jake said that because there was one piece of information he still had to reveal to Dana, which was that Joseph Harrison had left one last clue *within* the *Cross of Faith*, which Jake had kept before handing the treasures over to the government.

The clue revealed something bigger than Jake could ever imagine, so he knew that his adventures with Dana weren't over.

Dear Reader

Thank you for reading *Jake Raven and The Heists of Opulence*.

I was inspired to write this book by a short story I wrote in English class in high school. My philosophy behind this book was to provide a quicker read than usual but still one that had a big impact. I selfishly combined that philosophy with my favourite topic of treasure hunting, and this was the end result.

I poured my heart and soul into this book and uniquely made it mine, but now it's yours too.

I hope you enjoyed it. I hope you found admiration in the bond between Jake and Dana, and I hope I kept you on the edge of your seat, enthusiastically reading on to find out what happened in each chapter. But most of all, I hope the words of these pages helped you find what Jake and Dana had been sharing together all along; a sense of adventure and belonging.

Yours truly,
Gavin Kerst.

Sydney, Australia.
December 2020.

CPSIA information can be obtained
at www.ICGtesting.com
Printed in the USA
LVHW081752150121
676284LV00002BB/186